ABDUCTING ABBY

DRAGON LORDS OF VALDIER

BOOK 1

D1608137

BY S. E. SMITH

Acknowledgments

I would like to thank my husband Steve for believing in me and being proud enough of me to give me the courage to follow my dream. I would also like to give a special thank you to my sister and best friend Linda who not only encouraged me to write but who also read the manuscript.

—S. E. Smith

CHAPTER 1

Zoran Reykill pushed the body of the dead guard off him. He paused to draw in a sharp breath as pain sliced through his battered body. He had been in captivity for the past month, and there wasn't a place on his body that didn't hurt from the numerous cuts and bruises from the beatings and torture he had lived through. He forced himself to roll the guard over and pulled the guard's clothes off his body. His own clothes had been taken not long after he was brought down to the hell they called a cell. This was the first opportunity he had to escape. He had been watching and waiting for his captors to make a mistake, and they finally had, thinking he was too beaten down to fight. The guard Zoran had killed had come in to *play*, thinking he would relieve the boredom of standing guard over a chained prisoner by beating him some more. Instead, the guard found him hanging lifeless from the wall by his wrists and ankles. When the guard unlocked his wrists, Zoran had grabbed him, breaking his neck immediately, so he couldn't fight or call out. Zoran knew he would not have survived long in a fight. He was too weak. It took everything in him to push the guard off and find the release on the locking mechanism to release his ankles.

Struggling into the guard's clothes, he pulled the laser pistol and blade from the guard, checking to make sure both were fully charged. He reached down and yanked the security badge from the guard's neck. He knew it was late and there wouldn't be many guards about at this time of the night. Closing the solid door behind him, he moved down the darkened corridor. The dark did not bother him as he shifted to allow his night vision to take over. His people were renowned for their ability to adapt to the dark. As a dragon shifter, he felt the beast inside him straining to get out. He hadn't dared shift while in captivity. Without his symbiot to help shield him, he would have been too vulnerable. He fought to control his inner self as he moved through the prison maze. Even though he had only been half conscious when he was brought to the prison, he knew the way out, having played it over and over in his mind during the last month. Even if he hadn't been conscious, he would have smelled the night air as it called to him.

He was Zoran Reykill, leader of the Valdier. He was the most powerful of his kind, matched only by his brothers. He had been enjoying time on a remote planet on the outer rim of his own solar system, hunting and enjoying the favors of some of the women brought there for such things. Ordinarily, he would have by-passed pleasure, but he had been gone from his own world for two months on a diplomatic mission. He spent two days hunting in the thick forests of the planet before heading into the city complex. He did not suspect anything until after the meal, when he started to feel very lethargic. He only had time to send a message to his symbiot that he was in danger. He woke, chained in a Curizan spaceship. That was a month ago. The Curizans hoped to ransom him back after they obtained information about the symbiotic relationship his people enjoyed with a living metal organism capable of changing shape and harnessing enormous power. The relationship allowed his people to enjoy many attributes, including longevity, the ability to heal at a faster rate, and unbelievable space travel. Zoran was worried his symbiot would be captured and made sure it remained hidden until he could escape. He knew he would need it when the time came.

The Valdier lived on the outer rim of the Zion cluster of planets. Only in the past three hundred years had they developed a relationship with neighboring star systems. At first, the Valdier were very careful about who was allowed to visit. They were very protective of the interaction of their species with the symbiot. It was not until other species tried to capture and use the golden metal organism, only to have the symbiot attack and kill whatever species tried to touch it, that the Valdier felt more comfortable interacting with other species. This presented a problem, since there was not an abundance of females on Valdier, and the symbiot was not very tolerant of females from other species. It forced many males to limit their time with females who were not from their own planet. Zoran had yet to find a mate, although he had many females who could pleasure him should he desire a companion at the palace. The symbiot could live separate from the host for brief periods. His own symbiot divided so a small part of it could find him in the prison cell, healing his body and giving him enough strength to survive the beatings and torture. The symbiot then returned to the main body to replenish it with his essence. If not for that, both would have perished.

Now, he felt the strength of it calling to him. He rounded a corner near the entrance. Two guards stood talking quietly back and forth in the tongue of the Curizan. Zoran pulled the laser pistol and quickly disposed of both of them. He could only hope there were no other guards outside the entrance. Holding his ribs against the burning he felt, he swiped the guard's badge over the scanner and stood back as the door slid open. Peering outside, he moved into the shadows heading for the landing area. His symbiot was waiting for him there in the form of a space fighter. It took on the reflective surface making it invisible to all around it. It was only their connection that guided Zoran to it. Within moments, he was climbing into the cockpit of the Valdier fighter. With a wave of his hand, gold bands formed up his arms, sliding under his skin until he was one with the golden creature.

"Get us out of here," Zoran murmured softly, trying to hold onto consciousness. He was hurt much worse than he originally thought. He could feel the bones in his ribs rubbing against each other.

The symbiot glowed gold as it began rising out of the compound. Shouts and hisses erupted as the symbiot lost its cloak of invisibility. Moving smoothly, the golden fighter rose and moved out of the compound moving with blinding speed. Zoran knew he needed to stay conscious until he could find a safe place to land and let his body heal. Warnings sounded in his mind as Curizan fighters scrambled to pursue him. Zoran was not concerned, knowing that as soon as they reached the outer obit of the planet, his symbiot could move faster than the speed of light. Focusing on using defensive moves to get away from the pursuing fighters, he commanded the symbiot to plot a course to a quadrant of the galaxy unknown to the Curizan. He would never make it back to his own world in the shape he was in. He sent a message out to his brothers, hoping they would receive it before he lost consciousness. Zoran gave the final command to leap as soon as they cleared the planet's atmosphere. It was the last thing he remembered.

CHAPTER 2

Abby Tanner stared at the glass, seeing more in the hot glowing piece than molten liquid. As she began twirling the rod around and around she began forming different layers, bending and shaping them to match the image in her head. She loved how the shapeless glass transformed into a beautiful piece of art. She was also thankful she made a very good living from it. It gave her freedom that not many people could enjoy. She worked with the piece for the next three hours, blending and blowing until a delicate flower formed. She was almost finished. The piece she was working on had taken her almost six months to finish. She had already sold it for over fifty thousand dollars. For her, though, it was not the money but the enjoyment of creating something beautiful and enjoyed by others.

Abby looked up when she heard a dog bark. Smiling, she finished cleaning up her workshop. It was a fairly good size wooden barn not far from the cabin she lived in deep in the mountainous region of northern California. Her grandparents had lived in the cabin before she was born. When her mother took off when she was a baby it became her home. Her mother died of a drug overdose when Abby was two and she never knew her father. Her grandmother and grandfather had raised her. Her grandmother passed away five years ago and her grandfather six months ago. Abby still fought with the depression that overwhelmed her at times. Her grandparents were perfectly happy living in the remote mountain cabin. Abby grew up running through a wooded playground built just for her. She loved the freedom of the mountains and peace it gave her.

At twenty-two, she had no desire to live in the nearby town of Shelby or the larger cities. It was bad enough when she left to attend a gallery opening of her work. Brushing her dark brown hair that had fallen loose from her ponytail back behind her ears, Abby took another quick look around before closing the double doors to her workshop.

Laughing as the big golden retriever came running up to her, Abby bent down and gave Bo a big hug trying to keep her mouth shut so she didn't get Bo's overeager tongue in it.

"He misses you," Edna Grey said as she walked down the little path following Bo.

Edna had her long, dark gray hair in a braid down her back today instead of up in a bun. She was dressed in a pair of well-worn jeans with a plaid button up shirt tucked in at the waist. Even though she was in her late sixties, she moved like a woman half her age. Abby couldn't help but smile as she saw the twinkle in Edna's light green eyes as she followed Bo.

Abby glanced up at Edna and smiled. She could only hope she looked as good as her friend did when she got older. Abby knew she looked young even for her age. She gave credit for her appearance to her grandmother's side of the family. She had her grandmother's dark brown hair, dark blue eyes and heart-shaped face. Her nose was a little on the short side while her lips were a little on the full. Abby often thought the combination made her look like a pouty little girl but her grandfather used to say it made her even more beautiful because he could always see her grandmother in her.

"I missed him too. Yes, you are just a big ole softy, aren't you? Yes, you are," Abby said as she stood up.

Bo jumped back and forth waiting for Abby to pick up the tennis ball he was carrying in his mouth. His long tail swept back and forth as he pranced around in circles barking. Abby picked up the wet tennis ball and threw it toward the cabin. Like a bullet, Bo raced after the slime green prize.

"So, how are you doing?" Edna asked softly, walking back toward the cabin with Abby.

Abby was quiet for a moment before she let out a deep breath. "I'm doing better. It was really hard at first losing Granddad, but each day I seem to be handling it a little better. It helps being busy. That big piece I was working on for the couple from New York is almost done."

Edna put her arm around Abby's waist hugging her close. "I can't wait to see it. You've never been as secretive about any of your pieces as you have this one."

Abby laughed huskily. "It's one of the most beautiful pieces I've ever done. I can't wait for you to see it. When I was contracted to do the work I was a little hesitant. Normally, I just create based on what I feel is in the glass.

This time my client wanted to meet me and asked me to create something based on their home décor. I spent two days as a guest in their house. It was unbelievable. It helped. I was contracted to do it right after Granddad died. Being focused on it has helped me cope with his passing."

"Is there any chance of you meeting a nice young man while you are going back and forth in all your travels?" Edna teased.

"No, absolutely not!" Abby said, horrified. "I like being alone. I've seen enough of men and their behaviors on my trips to make me leery of getting involved with anyone."

"What about Clay? You know he's interested," Edna asked.

Abby wrinkled up her nose in distaste. Clay was the local sheriff for the town of Shelby and had been trying to get Abby to go out with him since she was eighteen. He was a nice guy, but Abby just didn't feel the same way about him as he seemed to feel about her. Abby made the weekly trip to town to mail the blown glass she sold to her distributors and pick up any items she needed, like groceries or supplies. And every week without fail, Clay would show up at the post office to ask her to go out with him. She would politely turn him down, and he would follow her around town bugging her to have a meal with him.

"Clay's a nice guy and all, but I just don't feel that way about him," Abby said, petting Bo and throwing the ball again.

"One day you'll meet the right man. Thank you again for keeping an eye on Gloria and Bo for me," Edna said as they walked up to the horse trailer attached to the back of her pickup truck.

"No problem. You know I enjoy their company when you take your little trips," Abby said with a laugh, watching as Gloria, Edna's old mule, tried to nudge her head out of the little window. Gloria loved the apples Abby always gave her.

"Well, you are the only one Gloria doesn't try to bite and push around." Edna opened the trailer and backed Gloria out. Bo danced around the old mule's feet trying to play.

"How long are you going to be gone?" Abby asked, pulling an apple out of the smock she wore over her shirt and jeans. "I hear there's a storm coming in tomorrow night that's supposed to be pretty bad." She held out the apple for Gloria who swept it out of her hand crunching on it as Edna led her over to the small corral near the cabin.

"Yeah, I heard about it. We're supposed to get a couple of inches of rain and possible severe thunderstorms. I plan on heading out as soon as I leave here so I can miss it. I'll be back by the end of the week. Jack and Shelly are having Crystal's birthday party on Thursday. I'll drive back on Friday," Edna said as she let Gloria go with a swat to her flanks.

"Do you have time for a cup of tea or coffee?" Abby asked, watching as Gloria walked into the small barn attached to the corral. Abby had already put down a thick bed of hay for Gloria in one of the stalls and had fresh food and water.

"A cup of coffee would be great," Edna said, following Abby up the steps and into the small cabin.

Abby loved her small home. It had two bedrooms, each with its own bathroom, a small living room, and a combination dining room/kitchen. A huge fireplace dominated the living room, and small pellet stoves occupied each bedroom for the chilly winter months. Luckily, it was getting to be early summer, so except for an occasional cool night she wouldn't need to light either the stoves or the fireplace. The cabin had large windows in the kitchen and living room, which let in an abundance of natural light.

Abby's grandfather owned his own music business in Los Angeles, and her grandmother had been a songwriter. Both had been extremely talented. When Abby's mom fell in with the wrong crowd, they thought moving to the mountains would get her away from it. Unfortunately, her mother ran away, instead, and at seventeen, she became pregnant with Abby. Abby had only been a month old when her mom dropped her off and disappeared. Two years later, she was found dead from a drug overdose along with her current boyfriend. Abby's grandparents were devastated by the death of their only daughter and did everything they could to make sure Abby was kept out of that type of life.

Abby had her grandmother's gentle personality and love for the arts. Her grandmother used the time in the mountains to write songs and taught herself the art of glass blowing. Soon, her grandfather had taken up the hobby, and it became another business with the help of the Internet. In the past six years, Abby had made a name for herself internationally with her beautiful creations.

Edna and Abby spent the next half hour catching up on Edna's family who lived in Sacramento and Abby's new contracts from several different museums asking to display her work. Bo was content to lie on the rug in front of the hearth watching his tennis ball. Before long, Abby was watching the taillights of Edna's pickup truck disappear down the steep driveway of her home. Abby called Bo to come back as he tried to follow Edna's truck, laughing as he looked back and forth, trying to decide who he wanted to stay with. A promise of a treat soon had him running back up the steps of the cabin and into the warm interior.

CHAPTER 3

Another bolt of lightning flashed, and then thunder rolled across the sky, shaking the cabin walls. The electricity had gone out over an hour ago, and Abby had lit a couple of candles to light the interior, although the way the lightning was flashing she probably didn't need to. Bo had taken refuge under the bed in her bedroom. Every once in a while she would hear him whine, and she would call out soft reassurances to him. Gloria was tucked up in the barn nice and safe. Abby hoped there wouldn't be too much damage but wasn't too optimistic from the sounds raging outside. She did what she could to prepare. Rain fell in sheets limiting the view outside to just a few feet. It was going to be a long night. Abby sat at the small table staring out the kitchen window when another bolt of lightning flashed. It was strange; but, she could have sworn there was something else in the thunder than followed. She caught a glimpse of something in the sky with that last flash.

Bo whined again, this time coming out from under the bed to put his head on Abby's knee. He still had his tennis ball in his mouth. Abby reached down and absently petted Bo's head, scratching behind his ears.

Sighing, Abby leaned over and dropped a soft kiss on the top of Bo's head, "Come on. Let's go to bed. Watching the storm isn't going to make it pass any faster, and I have a feeling there is going to be plenty of cleanup work to do tomorrow. Maybe we can find you a couple of sticks to carry back."

Abby stood up and blew out the candle on the table then picked up the one in the living room to carry with her into the bedroom. She brushed out her hair and changed into a pair of pajama pants and matching tank top that had little pictures of dogs on it. She climbed into the full-size bed and scooted over, patting next to her for Bo to jump up.

"You can help keep me warm tonight, big guy," Abby whispered as she wrapped an arm around the soft fur snuggled up against her.

* * *

The next morning was bright, and she saw that the storm had cleared
away everything in its path. Abby sipped a cup of coffee as she walked down
the front steps of the cabin. There were bits of limbs everywhere. A tree had
fallen behind the barn, but it hadn't done any damage. Bo ran down the steps
and raced around the yard smelling all the branches to see if the storm had
brought anything fun to play with. Abby opened the door to the barn and
moved to the stall holding Gloria. Gloria leaned her head over the door of the
stall looking droopy-eyed at Abby.

"Did the storm keep you up last night, girl?" Abby asked as she ran her
hand behind one of Gloria's ears then down along her jaw. "Come on, let's get
you outside to enjoy the beautiful weather."

Abby moved into the stall and opened the sliding door at the back of the
stall, which led into the corral. After making sure everything was still secure,
she picked up a brush and brushed Gloria before closing the gate.

"Come on Bo. Let's take a walk and see what else needs to be done," Abby
called as she moved down the path toward her workshop.

She would check it out before heading toward the meadow farther up the
mountain, where she had seen the weird light last night. She had dreamed
about it. She couldn't really remember much of her dream, just a nagging
feeling that she needed to check it out. Her workshop had survived the
storm just fine. She was glad, since she had several thousand dollars worth of
materials inside, not to mention the piece she was almost finished with. Bo
pranced around, wagging his tail and marking just about everything. Abby
laughed at the male need to mark. It reminded her a little of Clay when he
followed her around town glaring at anyone who looked her way.

Bo ran ahead down the path. Abby was a bit slower as she stopped to
move some of the bigger branches out of her way. She liked to hike up to the
meadow during the summers and just enjoy the scenery. She was lifting a
really large branch to the side when she heard Bo barking excitedly.

"Hold on, boy. I'm coming," Abby yelled. She pushed the limb out of the
way and jogged up the path.

Abby stopped suddenly, her mouth hanging open, as she stared at the
huge golden ship in the middle of the meadow. Bo was walking around it.
As he moved closer, the ship seemed to shudder and move away from him.
It was almost like it was alive. Abby moved slowly toward the golden ship.

"Bo, come here, boy. I think you're scaring it," Abby said softly.

Bo took one more sniff of the golden ship before taking off on another adventure. Abby walked around the ship, watching as it shivered when she stepped closer to it. It wasn't very big, maybe about the size of a large SUV, but it was absolutely beautiful. She looked at the sleek design. Different colors swirled through the outer coating, making the golden ship almost invisible as it took on the colors around it.

Abby slowly reached out to touch the ship's surface. It shimmered a bright gold, almost as if in warning. It reminded Abby of some of the wildlife she had seen up in the mountains. She and her grandparents sometimes came across frightened or wounded animals over the years and they nursed many back to health before releasing them back to the wild.

"It's okay, baby. I'm not going to hurt you," Abby whispered softly. "It's going to be all right."

The golden ship shuddered again as brushed her hand gently against its smooth surface. She laughed softly as she felt the smooth, soft metal. She didn't understand what it was or where it had come from, but she didn't get any bad vibes from it. She let her other hand glide over the surface, as well. She rubbed it lightly while whispering nonsense words. She felt her hands slowly sink into the soft metal, and long strips of the gold reached out, winding themselves around her arms and wrists. Abby's breath caught in her throat as she watched the gold bands slowly slide up her arms. When she pulled back, two thin, intricately designed gold bands were attached to her wrists like gold wrist cuffs. Abby stared at them, marveling at their beauty, as she ran her fingers over first one then the other.

Bo's sudden barking turned to a scared yelp as he charged back toward Abby. Abby moved away from the ship looking up startled as Bo raced past her toward the path leading back to her cabin. Turning toward where Bo had come from, Abby wondered what other wonders the storm had brought.

"Well, what got your tennis balls stirred up?" Abby asked bemused. She was still in a daze at finding something so beautiful on her mountain. A groan from the direction Bo had just run from caused Abby to take a step back.

* * *

Zoran groaned as he tried to lift his head. He didn't remember much about the landing. He knew he needed to get out; his body was on fire, but he didn't remember much but the fierce weather from the planet. He collapsed, unable to move, as the pain in his body overwhelmed him. He knew he needed to get back to his symbiot but didn't have the energy. He could only hope the message he sent out to his brothers would be received as darkness once again took him.

* * *

Abby bit her lip as she moved slowly toward the sound of the groan she had just heard. She really hoped this unexpected visit didn't turn out to be one of those horror-film/alien-possession things. She knew the golden ship was not from Earth. It didn't take a NASA scientist to figure that out. She just hoped curiosity didn't end up getting her killed. Abby saw the figure lying face down in the damp grass. Well, if it was an alien, he sure had the figure of a human—a very big human. Abby wasn't a shrimp at five-foot-eight, but this guy had to be well over six and a half feet if he was an inch.

Moving hesitantly until she stood next to him, she saw he had long black hair and was wearing some type of uniform with black epaulets on the shoulders. She couldn't see what his face looked like because his hair was covering it. She stooped down and gently brushed back his hair, letting her fingers rest for a moment on his neck. She found a weak pulse. What worried her the most, however, was how hot his skin felt. The gold on one of her wrists moved when she touched the man, turning to a liquid and pouring down her fingers until it wrapped around the man's throat. Abby was afraid at first that it meant to harm him, but then warmth flowed through her and she knew it wouldn't.

"I don't know what you are, but I don't get the feeling you want to hurt him either," Abby murmured under her breath. "Let's see what our man looks like and what we can do to help him out."

Abby ran her hands down the figure looking for any obvious signs of trauma before gently rolling him over onto his back. She drew in a deep breath. He was the most handsome man she had ever seen in her life. He was also the most beat up man she had ever seen. How someone could hurt another being like this broke Abby's heart. Blood spotted his uniform on both the front and the back, making it obvious that the uniform had been put on over the injuries since it was not cut up. His facial features were definitely human-like. Abby ran her fingers over his face, gently touching the cuts above his left eye and cheek before moving down to his lips. He had strong, proud features. His nose was a little broader than normal, and he had prominent cheekbones, much like the Native American Indians. His color was similar too with the darker tanned skin. She wondered what color his eyes would be—brown, blue, or almost black—but they were closed, and she did not want to force them open.

Abby checked him over to see if he had any broken bones. She worried about his ribs, since even in his unconscious state, he jerked when she probed them. She realized the only way she was going to be able to get him to the cabin was on a skid. She whistled for Bo to come to her. He had taken off toward the cabin earlier, but she had seen him sniffing around the meadow again a few minutes ago.

Bo wagged his tail as he came toward Abby, keeping his head down and his eyes nervously on the still figure next to her. "Come on, boy. I need you to be a guard dog and protect our visitor until I get back with Gloria," Abby said petting the golden retriever behind the ear.

"Stay," Abby commanded Bo and watched as he lay down next to the man, letting his resting his head on the man's chest. "Good boy. Stay."

Abby took off at a run for her cabin. She would use the old skid she used to haul wood to bring the injured man back to the cabin. She quickly pulled out the harness gear and called Gloria over to her. She hooked up the skid behind Gloria and pulled some thick pads from the storage room of the barn and laid it on top of the skid. With a click of her tongue, Abby and Gloria moved up the path again to the meadow. Gloria was a pro at this, since Edna would bring her several times a year for Abby to use. It was too cold most of the winter to keep a horse or a mule up this high in the mountains; plus, there was not enough pasture land, so it was a win-win situation for Abby to just borrow Gloria when she needed the extra help.

Abby jumped off the skid once they entered the meadow. The gold ship glimmered as Abby walked by with Gloria. Abby couldn't help but run her hand along the ship's surface again to caress it.

"It's going to be okay. I'm going to help him. Then you can have him back. He just needs some TLC. I won't hurt him," Abby said as her fingers glided from the tip of the ship to the very back. She could almost feel the ship's sigh of relief at her words.

Bo looked up from his place next to the man. After fifteen minutes of grunting and pushing, Abby finally had the man on the padded skid. She was breathing heavily and sweating from the exertion.

"Wow. He's a lot bigger and heavier than I thought," Abby said to no one in particular. She didn't know if the ship, Bo, or Gloria really gave a damn about how big and heavy the man was.

Abby made the short trip back to the cabin at a much slower pace, aware of how the man groaned with every rut she hit. She would have to use the ramp her grandfather had built for her grandmother to get him into the cabin. The skid was narrow enough to fit through the front door of the cabin thanks to the extra wide door her grandfather had installed after her grandmother needed to use a wheelchair to get around. It would be tricky getting him in the room and in the bed but she felt sure she could do it with a little manipulation.

An hour later, totally exhausted, Abby lay on the bed next to the man. She had pushed, pulled, and tugged until she could barely move but she had him in the bed. She gave herself a few minutes to regroup before sitting up. First things first, she needed to get his clothes off so she could see the damage. Then she would bathe him and doctor his cuts.

Abby didn't want to cut the man's clothes up, but she found it was going to be the only way to get them off. The cloth was stuck to his skin by dried blood in many places and was stretched across him like a second skin in others. She would go to town later and get him some clothes, once she knew it was safe to leave him. As she cut the shirt off of him, Abby noticed the gold on the man's throat had moved down to his chest now. It just lay there curled up as if it was asleep. Abby couldn't contain the tears that filled her eyes at the number of cuts and bruises on the poor man. She tried not to blush when she got to his pants. He wasn't wearing anything under them and was just as impressive there as he was everywhere else. Abby did her best to keep her touch impersonal and hoped the man wouldn't be offended when he woke up and realized she had taken such liberties. His legs were covered with bruises as well as small cuts. It was as if he had been tortured. She gasped as she saw the deep cuts around his ankles. Her gaze flew to his wrists and, sure enough, he had deep cuts there as well. Whoever hurt the man had obviously had him shackled so he couldn't defend himself.

Abby threw the clothes into a pile. She would burn them later in the burn barrel behind the cabin. In the bathroom, she filled a bucket with lukewarm water. She needed to get his temperature down. She was afraid to give him any medication for a human, not knowing if it would hurt him. She hoped cleaning the wounds and bringing his temperature down would help. She rolled him onto his side and laid a vinyl tablecloth down with the plastic facedown so she wouldn't soak the mattress. She then laid several towels under him. She bathed his back first, just dampening his hair as best she could. She wouldn't be able to really wash it, but at least it would feel better than it had. As she bathed him she was careful to make sure she paid close attention to his cuts. It was strange watching the small gold band moving over his body as she moved the man. It seemed to go to the worse cuts and bruises and stay there for a few moments before moving on. Once, it even came to her and wrapped around her wrist while the other gold wrist cuff dissolved and moved to replace it. Abby just shivered when she felt them move over her. It wasn't a bad feeling. In fact, it felt warm and fuzzy.

Abby turned even redder as she washed the man's private area. He was thickly built and long even in his relaxed state. She had never seen or touched a man before, and her hands shook as she gently cleaned him. She was thankful he was unconscious and would never know what she had done. She tried to think what a nurse would do in such a situation. Hell, she knew even some cosmetologists worked with peoples' private areas. She tried to focus on the gold band moving up and over the man's body from one place to another. She watched in fascination as cuts began to heal right before her eyes wherever the gold band touched. Right now, it was working on his right wrist.

Once Abby was done, she removed the damp tablecloth and towels and covered the man with the thick quilt. She put him in her grandparents' old bedroom. The bed was a king size and seemed to fit him better than her full-size bed. She felt his forehead again, and it felt a little cooler. His complexion looked better as well. She had enough time to put Gloria in the pen and make some dinner before dark. The electricity was still off, and she didn't want to run the generator any more than she had to. She could measure the man and order him some clothes from the Internet. Luckily, her laptop was fully charged, and she used satellite for her connection since no service ran this far up into the mountains.

An hour later, Abby closed the laptop satisfied with her order. She had ordered several shirts and pairs of pants, boxers, socks, and after measuring his feet, which she found were ticklish, a pair of boots and a pair of tennis shoes. It wasn't easy finding both in a size eighteen wide. She stood up and stretched. The gold bands had switched again, and she noticed the one on her left wrist seemed to be stroking her. Abby smiled as she gently rubbed the little gold band. She could tell it seemed to enjoy it when she did that. She figured she would sleep in the big bed next to the man tonight. There was plenty of room for her skinny butt, and this way, if the gold bands needed to change they could. Plus, she just felt better staying close to him. At least until he woke up.

CHAPTER 4

Zoran stretched, waiting for the pain to slice through his body. He kept his eyes closed as he sent out his senses to determine what dangers might be close at hand. When he didn't feel the normal wrenching of pain, he froze. He could feel his symbiot moving around his body repairing the damage. Had he found shelter? He frowned; he couldn't remember. Had his brothers found him? He did not detect their presence. He did a quick internal review. His ribs were healed, though still tender, and the numerous cuts and bruises were also healed. He felt clean, but he did not remember bathing. He also realized he was completely nude beneath a soft thick covering. He didn't recognize any of the scents around him as being from his home.

He let his senses expand to cover the room. He was alone in the room but not in the structure. There were two other species in it with him. While he did not recognize the scents, they were vaguely familiar. He heard a soft, pleasant sound, a type of soft singing coming from the other room before he heard the sound of footsteps as they approached him.

Abby sang softly under her breath as she prepared a vegetable broth for her guest. She had been forcing the broth down his throat for the past two days, fearful of him becoming dehydrated or malnourished. The electricity had come back on late last night. She was thankful, since she needed to finish the piece she was working on, and it was just safer not using candles. Pouring the broth into a deep bowl, she set it on the tray. She hoped her guest woke up soon. If he didn't wake up by tomorrow, she was going to have to call for the doctor to come look in on him. She went up to the meadow twice a day as well to pet and talk to the gold ship. She didn't know why, but she had a feeling it was worried about the man. She was rewarded with another gold bracelet, necklace, and earrings. At the rate she was going, she would be so loaded down she wouldn't be able to walk.

Abby walked quietly into the bedroom. The mid-morning sun shone brightly through the large windows.

"Good morning, sleeping beauty. I've made you some more of that delicious broth you love so much. How about opening those gorgeous eyes and giving me a peek at who's sleeping his life away? Bo would love to have someone to play catch with, and your golden ship seems to be missing you as well." Abby kept up the running monologue she had started yesterday morning, thinking that if he heard someone's voice he might respond faster. The Internet said people in a coma could hear what people said, so maybe this hunk of a man could hear her.

Zoran frowned as the translator imbedded in his brain took a moment to learn and translate the words the creature spoke. He breathed in deeply to catch the creature's scent and was immediately hit by the fragrance of sunlight, woods, and wildflowers. His body jerked in response, his cock filling with need as the beast inside him responded to the female. His fingers clenched under the covers as he fought the overpowering reaction to the female's voice and scent.

He could tell she was not a Valdier. Her scent was wrong, but it was also right. He had never had such a powerful reaction to any of the females on his planet, or any other, for that matter.

He heard her set something on the table next to him before the bed sank down slightly from her weight. He bit back a groan as he felt her soft fingers slide through his hair and down along his face caressing him.

"Come on, fly boy. Don't you want to wake up? It's such a beautiful day outside. I need to go into town today, and I don't like leaving you alone when you are so defenseless." Abby enjoyed running her fingers through his long hair and along his jaw.

Suddenly, strong tan fingers wrapped around her fragile wrist and she was jerked over his body until she was lying on her back under a huge chest. Abby let out a squeal as she was flipped over the long, hard body of the male who moments before had been totally still and unresponsive. She lay still, staring up into dark gold eyes. Her breath caught in her throat as she stared into the strong, fierce face of a man who could snap her neck between his fingers if he felt like it.

Zoran stared down into the face of the female lying beneath him. She was stunningly beautiful. Her eyes were a dark blue with little flakes of black in them. She lay perfectly still beneath him as he studied her. Her eyes were open wide but they did not show any fear. It was like she was waiting for him to make up his mind what needed to be done next. He held one of her slim wrists in his large hand, while he pressed her other hand against his bare chest. He felt her fingers move, spreading out so they wove in the dark hairs covering his chest. He shivered as he felt her short nails scrape him lightly. His body tightened with need. He wanted her. It wasn't until he bent to kiss her wrist that he noticed the gold symbiot wrapped tightly around it. His gaze jerked down to her throat where her pulse beat a fast tempo. A small glimmer of gold showed from her throat, as well as from her ears and her other wrist. How was it possible? She was not of their species but his symbiot had claimed her.

Jerking up into a sitting position, Zoran gripped the shirt covering the female and jerked it down ripping the buttons off. Abby cried out, startled, and tried to pull away. Zoran pulled her roughly to his chest pinning her to him as he moved his hand to her throat and his symbiot. He buried his nose in her throat, listening to her frantic heart beat as his fingers gently touch his symbiot. He communicated with it making sure the female had not harmed it. If she had, he would break her neck. The warmth that flooded him took his breath away. Not only had the female cared for him but she had also cared for the mother symbiot, which was his ship. Zoran saw flashes of her stroking and reassuring his symbiot that it was safe and that she was going to take care of him. He saw the way she struggled to take him back to her home, how she bathed him, fed him, and held him at night talking to him softly. He felt a wave of desire so intense, he wanted to take her right then and there, claiming her as his, because, whether she realized it or not, she *was* his. His symbiot recognized his true mate right away and his body recognized her as soon as he awoke.

Abby waited fearfully to see what the man was going to do. She knew he could snap her neck in a heartbeat if he wanted too. When he tore her shirt open, she feared he would do worse. She would not let him or any other man rape her without a fight. As the minutes passed and he did nothing, she began to relax. She could feel him running his finger over the gold at her neck and figured he must have reacted to seeing it, other than a desire to take her body. She had to admit she was a little disappointed. She had been fighting lustful thoughts ever since she found him.

"If you are going to kill me then please get it over with; otherwise, can you let me up as your brunch is getting cold?" Abby said calmly.

Zoran looked down into Abby's eyes again before he seemed to realize he still held her tightly against him. Reluctantly, he released her, helping her into a sitting position.

Abby smiled gently while trying to hold her blouse together. She blushed when she saw his eyes follow her movement, and she felt her nipples swell in response. She turned even redder when she saw the desire come into his eyes, as if he knew her response to him.

Abby scooted to the side of the bed away from him and stood up. "Do you understand me?"

Zoran watched carefully as the female moved hesitantly around the end of the bed. He knew she wanted to escape but he had no desire to let her leave his sight. "*Zi.*"

Abby frowned. He seemed to understand her but she didn't understand what he was saying. "*Zi.* Is that yes?"

"*Zi.*" Zoran said with a frown. Didn't her translator work?

Abby sighed as she moved toward the door. "I need to put on a new shirt. I'll be back in a minute." Abby whirled around to leave, only to find herself caught up against his broad chest, again, a very broad, naked chest and something suspiciously long poking her in the back.

"Oh, dear," Abby whispered, closing her eyes as she felt the arms tighten around her. "I...I promise, if you let me go, I'm just going into the next room to get another shirt. I...I'll be right back."

Zoran bent his head to run his lips along the female's neck. He could feel her heart fluttering as she tried to hold herself still. He let one of his hands move until it pressed between her breasts over her heart.

"Please don't hurt me." Abby whispered hoarsely.

Zoran frowned when he heard her softly spoken words. She was afraid of him. He felt her body begin to shake. He did not mean to frighten her. He just wanted to prevent her from leaving his sight. The symbiot moved around the female's neck to wind around his wrist. He felt a slight shock, as if it was warning him to be careful. He jerked his hand back, staring in shock. Never had his symbiot behaved this protectively against him.

Abby felt his hand move away from her and jerked away, turning and holding her hand out to stop the man from advancing on her. It wasn't until then that she realized he was standing completely nude in front of her. Not only was he nude, but he had a very impressive hard-on. Abby blushed a bright red, her eyes widening as she jerked her gaze up to the man's face.

"Oh dear," Abby said putting a hand over her eyes as she tried to back up. She felt behind her until she found the doorframe and moved in jerky steps until she was clear and could run for her bedroom.

Zoran watched as the female in front of him jerked away, her eyes widening as she took in his state of undress and her face flushed a bright pink. She looked adorable with her wide blue eyes and lush rounded lips. Just as quickly, she covered her eyes with one hand while feeling her way out the door with the other. Zoran did not understand why she felt the need to cover her eyes. His people were quite comfortable with their bodies, and the females often walked around without clothing while inside. He felt a soft chuckle escape as he became aware the female was totally unaware that when she covered her eyes and felt for the doorway, she left her torn shirt open for him to observe her body. A thin lacy cloth covered her full breasts that he found very arousing, as it pushed her breasts up and only a hint of her colorful nipples were visible. She had a full figure with a small waist and hips made for grabbing. He felt himself growing harder as she moved away from him. He took a step toward her, watching as she twirled around and disappeared through a door into the next room.

Zoran moved into what looked like a living area of the female's house. Another creature lay on a rug chewing on a bone of some type. It was small compared to most of the creatures he was familiar with and had golden fur all over it. It wagged its tail as it looked at him with large brown eyes. A green ball lay next to it. The home was small but was very comfortable with simple furnishings. He waited until the door opened to the room next to him and watched as the female came out of it wearing another shirt, this one with no opening on the front. She was pulling her hair out from the back when she stopped suddenly looking at him.

"You..." Abby gulped. "You need to get some clothes on. You can't walk around nude."

Zoran raised an eyebrow at the sound of command in the female's voice. She did not like him walking around naked? He looked down. He was not bad to look at. Many females would give much to be in his home and in his bed. Why did the female not like him unclothed? Was he so different from the males of her species? He felt a burst of jealousy at the thought of the female with another male. She was his. He glared at her.

"Come on. I'll show you where the shower is and you can get cleaned up and dressed. I'll fix you something a little more filling than the broth."

Abby moved nervously around the man standing in her living room. God, she had never seen a more handsome male. Why did he have to be from so far away?

Zoran followed Abby into the bathroom. He listened as she explained how the shower worked, how the toilet worked, and where the towels were. She had laid out sweat pants that belonged to her grandfather and a T-shirt. She figured they would be a little short and big on him but at least he would be covered. She said she had ordered him some clothes and they should be in. She would go to town later to pick them up. She had them shipped "overnight," whatever that meant. She never looked at him directly as she explained everything and tried to keep as much distance as she could between them in the small space. When she was done, she quickly turned, closing the door after her, saying she would be in the kitchen fixing lunch.

A bemused smile crossed Zoran's face. The female moved around much like the small flying creatures in the forest, which went from one flower to another, never staying still long enough to be caught. She aroused him with her sweet smell and the nervous glance in her dark blue eyes. He wondered if they would change colors when he made love to her. Turning on the shower, he closed his eyes as the warm water poured over his sore muscles. He connected with his symbiot asking it to replay her bathing him. He could almost feel her hands gently washing his battered body. When it replayed her washing his genitals, he felt his manhood flood with desire. Gripping his cock, he began pumping it, imagining her hands wrapped around it. He let out a loud groan as he swelled before he crested, spurting his hot seed in the shower. He braced an arm against the side while he gently stroked his cock. He shuddered feeling some relief but he wanted the female—badly.

Stepping out of the shower, he stared at his image in the reflective glass. He was nearly healed of the cuts and bruises. His ribs were still sore but he could feel they no longer rubbed where they had been broken. His face turned dark as he thought of the revenge he would seek against the men who had captured him. He would kill them all. They had not learned anything from him, but he knew if he did not make an example of them, others would try to gain knowledge about his people from others of his kind. It was his duty to protect his people. He sent out a command to his symbiot ship to let it know he was safe. He asked if it received word from his brothers yet. With a nod, he smiled. He would soon be returning home.

CHAPTER 5

Abby was just setting the table when her strange guest appeared. She let out a sigh of relief when she noticed he was dressed. The clothes hung on him, and the pants were more like long shorts than pants but at least he was covered.

Abby smiled and motioned for him to sit down at the table. "I hope you don't mind something simple. I don't have any meat in the house. I'm a vegetarian. I made you one of my special veggie burgers with some chips. Would you like iced tea? It's unsweetened, but I have sugar if you want sweet tea, milk, water, or coffee?"

Zoran frowned as he listened. He understood part of what she said. He wondered how she could not have meat in her home. Was she too poor or did she not have a man to hunt for her? He watched as she stood looking at him with wide, nervous eyes. His eyes were drawn to her lips. She was biting her lower lip as she stared at him. He moved slowly toward the table and sat hiding a smile when she suddenly let out her breath.

"I would like what you drink," Zoran replied in his language, waiting for the female to respond.

When she frowned at him again, he felt a flash of frustration. He was able to understand her perfectly but she seemed to not understand him. He pointed to the glass in front of her and then to his. Understanding lit up her face as she smiled at him showing off a set of dimples in each cheek that had Zoran groaning with pleasure as her face transformed. She was breathtaking when she smiled. Her eyes lit with an inner light, and she seemed to glow. Reaching over, Abby poured iced tea into his glass.

"It really is very good," Abby said hesitantly, nodding to the sandwich on his plate. "I guess I should introduce myself. My name is Abigail Tanner but everyone calls me Abby. This is my home." Nodding toward Bo who was sound asleep on the rug, she added, "That is Bo. He is the one who found you. He is visiting me for a few days while a friend of mine is visiting her family."

Zoran watched as Abby spoke softly. He liked the sound of her voice. It was soft and husky and made him think of wild things and warm sheets.

"I am called Zoran," Zoran said pointing to himself before he picked up the sandwich. He took a sniff of it before taking a bite. His eyes widened, as he tasted the blend of spices. It was unlike anything he had ever eaten before but was very good. He took another bite nodding his head as he chewed.

Abby smiled again. "Zoran. Welcome to my home," Abby said softly.

They spent the next hour trying to communicate. Abby was puzzled how Zoran could understand everything she said, but she couldn't understand him. When she asked about it, he pointed to his ears and said a word. Abby finally figured out it was some type of device that translated what she was saying. When she pointed to the gold bands around his wrist and the one around his neck he said something else she couldn't understand. Abby felt like she was playing a one-sided game of charades. It was very frustrating for her and she felt for him, as he wanted to ask her questions but she didn't understand what he was asking.

Bo finally decided it was time to go outside, and Abby got up from the table to let him out only to be pinned to Zoran's broad chest again. Abby looked up into the dark gold eyes, wondering what she had gotten herself into. Abby flushed when she saw the dark look of warning in Zoran's eyes.

"It's okay. Bo needs to go outside, and I need to check on Gloria. No one else is here. I live alone. Would you like to see where I found you? We still have plenty of daylight if you would like to go up to the meadow where your ship is." Abby stared up at the man who held her so tightly.

"Zi." Zoran was confused. Why did someone as lovely as Abby live alone? Surely it was too dangerous for her to be left unprotected. Who took care of her? Who made sure she had food and supplies?

Abby pressed her hands against Zoran's chest until he loosened his hold on her. Turning, she called out to Bo. Abby opened the door to the cabin, pausing briefly to give him a reassuring smile, before walking outside.

Zoran gazed around at the lush vegetation surrounding the cabin. He followed Abby over to a small fenced-in area watching as she called to a dark brown creature. He watched as Abby held out a small fruit to the creature that swept it out of her hand and crunched on it lazily.

"This is Gloria. She belongs to my friend Edna. She helped me bring you here from the meadow. She's such a good girl, aren't you Gloria? Yes, you are," Abby murmured as she scratched the creature behind its ear.

"I'll show you the meadow first. I'm sure you are worried about your ship. It's strange but I swear it seems like it is alive. I could feel it responding to me when I touched it. It was worried about you." Abby flushed as she looked up at Zoran, thinking he was going to think she was nuts. "I know that sounds stupid, but it was just a weird feeling I got."

Zoran had no way of explaining to Abby that his ship was, indeed, alive and was a part of him. He could feel it every time she would gently stroke the symbiot on her wrists. It was like she was stroking him. He felt her doing it several times inside her home, and she was doing it now as they walked along the path. He shivered as her fingers gently ran back and forth over the gold bracelets. Reaching down, he grabbed her hand preventing her from doing it any longer. If she didn't stop, he wouldn't be able to prevent himself from taking her right there on the path. Abby looked up startled but kept her hand in Zoran's larger one. They walked in a comfortable silence along the path. When they reached the meadow, Zoran released Abby's hand and marched over to the gold ship murmuring to it as he ran his hand over it. Abby watched in wonder as steps formed on the side and Zoran climbed into the ship. It was like something out of a science-fiction movie. Abby stood unsure of what to do. She didn't feel like she could leave him and didn't feel right climbing into the ship. She decided she would find a nice dry rock to sit on and wait. She still needed to go into town. If she left within the next hour she would be back before it got dark since it took so long to drive to town and back. Otherwise, she would have to leave early tomorrow morning. She still needed to finish the piece she was working on and between the storm and her unexpected visitor, she was behind her self-imposed schedule to have it done by the time Edna got back.

* * *

Zoran felt a huge sense of relief as he checked his symbiot. It survived the month of hiding and the sudden departure with minimal damage. Abby unknowingly helped to heal it. When she touched it, she gave a part of her essence to it, giving it the needed strength to heal. He watched the images flash through his mind as his symbiot replayed how Abby came twice a day, spending close to an hour just talking to it. She would run her hands all over it as she stroked it while whispering words of reassurance. He heard her talk about him. She had been worried about him. She was afraid he might not recover and afraid of having to call someone to come look at him. She didn't want others of her species to know about him because it would be too dangerous. She told his symbiot she was doing everything she could to help him and would protect him from harm until he was strong enough to leave. She did not understand, however, that he would not be leaving alone. He had no intentions of leaving her behind. Pushing what he was going to have to do out of his mind, he focused on opening communications with his brothers. He knew they should be close and wanted to warn them of the possible hostile environment.

"Zoran!" Kelan called out. An image of his brother's warship came into view. His symbiot was curled up in the shape of a huge golden cat near his chair.

"Kelan." Zoran paused to clear his throat. He feared he would never see his brothers again. "How long before you intercept?"

"We should be there in seven days' time. We have been monitoring communications from this galaxy. They only have one planet in this solar system that is habitable and do not appear to have space travel," Kelan responded.

"Who else is with you?" Zoran asked.

"Trelon. Mandra remained behind under protest. Creon is gathering intelligence on those who captured you and supervising plans to attack them."

"I am transmitting my position. It is remote. Come in using caution. This planet is not familiar with other species," Zoran said, sending the information.

"Information received. It is very primitive there. Soon you will be enjoying our home world's luxuries again," Kelan said. "It is good to see you are safe, Brother. Until we meet in seven days. *V'ager*, out."

Zoran acknowledged he would be at this site in seven days' time. He felt a wave of relief at the knowledge he would soon be on his way home. He missed his world, and he knew his symbiot did also. Moving out of the ship, Zoran felt a moment of panic when he did not see Abby. He sent a call out to his symbiot attached to her and felt relief when it replied it was close. He followed the call until he came upon Abby sitting on a large boulder with her eyes closed.

Abby had been sitting for about fifteen minutes when the combination of the sun's warmth and the relief from the stress of wondering if her visitor was going to be okay swept through her, making her drowsy. She hadn't had much sleep since the storm blew through three days before. Now, she just wanted to curl up and take a nap. She felt herself drifting, not really asleep but not awake either. She dreamed she was being lifted into Zoran's strong arms and his lips were brushing against hers. She moaned as she felt the warmth of his body and lips against her. She raised her arm to wrap it around his neck, pulling him further down when he moved away.

It took a moment for Abby to realize it was not a dream but that she was really kissing Zoran. Then it dawned on her that she was no longer on the rock but lying in his arms. Abby's eyes popped open, and she gasped as she stared into Zoran's golden eyes.

Zoran took advantage of Abby's startled gasp, letting his tongue slide between her lips. He deepened the kiss, as he felt Abby's fingers thread through his hair and pull him closer. By the time he pulled back, Abby was staring at Zoran with a dazed expression on her face and breathing heavily.

"Wow. I wasn't expecting that!" Abby whispered, unable to look away at first. Then, as she realized what she had said, she turned her face into his chest and groaned.

"I can't believe I just said that. Please let me go. I must have taken a cat-nap." Abby was mortified by her behavior. She had never behaved so wantonly before.

Pushing against Zoran's chest, Abby looked everywhere but at him. "Were you able to contact your family?"

Zoran frowned. He had not said anything about his family. How could Abby have known he was contacting them? A dark suspicion flashed through his mind that Abby might be a part of the Curizans' plans to get more information out of him. He had been unconscious since his arrival. Was it possible they were staging this in an attempt to get him to talk? Or worse, to capture his brothers? Zoran's arms tightened around Abby to the point of pain. He had no way of asking her unless she really did understand him and was just pretending not to.

"Ow! You're hurting me," Abby said, struggling to get free. Zoran's fingers just tightened even more on her arms. "Ouch, Zoran. Please, you're hurting me."

Abby looked up into Zoran's furious face, tears of pain in her eyes. "What's wrong? Why are you so angry with me?"

"What do you know of my family?" Zoran demanded in a harsh voice. "Are you working with the Curizans? Tell me now and I will spare your life; if you do not, I will show you no mercy when I kill you."

Abby just looked at Zoran with a confused and frightened look. "Zoran, please...I don't understand. What did I do to upset you?"

Zoran felt a wave of frustration. He did not sense Abby was lying to him, but how had she known his family was coming for him? Suddenly, both of the symbiot on Abby's wrist moved up under his hands and flashed him a shock that knocked him back off the rock and onto the ground.

Abby looked on in stunned disbelief as the two gold bracelets around her wrists suddenly moved with lightning speed to strike out at Zoran. When she felt the shock reach through him and saw him falling backwards she cried out in alarm. She didn't understand why he was so mad at her, and yes, he had frightened her, but she didn't want to see him get hurt.

Crying out, she reached out to him, her gaze moving back and forth between Zoran and the gold bracelets on her wrists. "Please don't hurt him. He didn't mean to hurt me. Please."

Abby turned tear-filled eyes to look at Zoran as he stood up, frowning at her as the symbiot moved back down around her wrists.

"I don't know why they did that. I didn't ask them too. I..." Abby brushed a tear from her cheek. "I thought you were trying to see if your people were coming for you. That's what I would do if I were you. I didn't mean to make you mad or hurt you."

Zoran felt a rush of shame flash through his body as he heard the truth of Abby's words. She had not known what he was doing. She just guessed that he would be contacting his family. He should have known that his symbiot would never have gone to her, *claimed* her, if she meant to harm him. It would have known if she was doing anything that would betray him.

Zoran stood for a moment unsure of what to do. He wanted to apologize for his behavior but knew Abby wouldn't understand what he was saying. Running his hand through his long hair, he looked at her with regret in his eyes. Spreading his palms out to show he meant her no harm, he tried to explain.

"I apologize for my behavior. I should have known you meant no harm to me," Zoran said softly.

Abby didn't know what Zoran was saying, but she could tell he regretted his behavior. She gave him a tentative smile to let him know no harm was done. She couldn't really blame him for being suspicious. If she had been beaten as badly as him, she would probably be afraid and suspicious too.

She gripped his hand and gave it a squeeze. "It's okay. I understand. If I had been in your position, I probably would have reacted the same way. I need to go to town to get my mail and pick up some supplies. Would you like to stay here with your ship or back at the cabin?"

Zoran frowned. He did not want Abby out of his sight. The thought of her traveling to a town made him nervous. He wanted her with him. Shaking his head, he frowned at her and motioned that she should stay with him.

Abby shook her head. "I need to go to town. I go at least once a week, sometimes twice if I have additional packages to mail off. If I don't go, someone might come looking for me. I don't think it would be a good idea for you to go with me. You don't have the right clothes and just the fact you are a stranger is going to cause people to notice you. I won't be gone long, a few hours. I'll be back before dark."

Zoran's lips thinned at the idea of Abby leaving, but he understood what she was saying. If he did not let her go, others of her kind might get suspicious and come looking for her. He needed to remain hidden for the next seven days. With a reluctant nod, he motioned for Abby to walk back to her cabin.

CHAPTER 6

Abby had been gone for the past five hours. Zoran was frustrated at her insistence to go alone. He walked with her down to a building containing an oddly shaped transport. She assured him she would be perfectly safe and asked him to keep an eye on Gloria and Bo for her until she returned. She explained where he could find food and drink, showed him how to operate a thing called a microwave, and gave him a remote if he wanted to listen to music. She apologized for not having a thing called a TV, explaining she didn't care to watch it but he could look at the computer if he wanted.

Zoran returned to his ship instead to contact his brother Creon. They discussed his captivity and plans for attacking the Curizan military base where he had been held. He also communicated again with Kelan and Mandra about what had happened and the trade agreements he had finalized before his captivity. They would be trading some of their crystals for women to supplement the needs of the men on his planet.

* * *

Abby laughed as she pulled down the driveway for the forty-minute ride to town. She was beginning to wonder if Zoran was ever going to let her leave. She went over all the things she could think of in the house to make sure he didn't starve while she was gone, but it took even longer to convince him she didn't need protection against whatever imaginary creatures he thought she might encounter. He wanted her to take some type of weapon he had with her and was mad as hell when she laughed and said she didn't need it. Now, she was running even later and would have to stop at the post office first if she wanted to get there before it closed.

Abby rolled down the window after she got on the highway and turned up the volume on the CD player, singing as she drove. She actually enjoyed the drive to town along the winding roads. The scenery was beautiful, and the weather was perfect. She made it to town with a half hour to spare before the post office closed and pulled into a spot right up front. She had no sooner turned off the engine to her pickup truck when Clay's sheriff's truck pulled in next to her.

Abby let out a frustrated sigh. She swore he had cameras set up to monitor for her arrival in town. Otherwise, there was no way he could know she was headed in. She really didn't want to deal with his advances today. She wanted to get her mail, stock up on some food, and get home as soon as possible. It was weird, but she already missed being with Zoran.

"Hey, Abby," Clay said, getting out of his truck and walking over to where Abby was locking her own vehicle.

"Hi, Clay, how's it going?" Abby asked as she moved toward the post office.

"Good. I'm glad to see you were able to get out after that storm the other night," Clay said, holding the door open for her.

"Thanks. Yeah, it was pretty bad, but it didn't take long for the electric company to get the power back on. I was expecting it to be much worse than it was," Abby said moving to her post office box.

"Did you have any damage? I can come up to your place and help you clean up if you need me," Clay said, watching as Abby pulled out her mail, picking out the green notices of boxes to pick up, and stuffing the rest of it in her bag without looking at it.

"No, no damage. A tree fell behind the barn but it didn't hit anything. There were some smaller branches lying around, but it won't take long to clear those up. I need to pick up some stuff. It was nice seeing you," Abby said, hoping Clay would take the hint and leave.

"I'll help you. How about going to the diner and getting something to eat when you're done?" Clay asked following Abby to the counter.

Abby let out a soft sigh. Nope, he wasn't going to leave her be. "Sorry, can't. I need to get back home before dark. You know I don't like driving at night."

It was the same excuse she had been giving Clay for the past four years. Their conversation could have been recorded, since it usually went the same. Clay would ask her out, she would give him an excuse, he would follow her around trying to change her mind, and she would smile and say maybe another time.

"Hi, Mrs. Patterson, how is Harry?" Abby said to the postal clerk, pushing the green notices toward Alicia Patterson. She had been the postmaster for Shelby probably since the beginning of time and was the number one person to see for any gossip. The woman had to be at least eighty.

"Harry's fine, dear. Thanks for asking. Are you going to be in town for the festival this year? We so look forward to listening to you sing," Mrs. Patterson said as she reached under the counter to pull out the boxes. "Strange to be getting men's clothing in the mail. Haven't seen any of this since your grandfather passed on. Are you seeing someone, dear?'

Abby gritted her teeth. She should have known Mrs. Patterson would have noticed where the items were coming from. Now everyone in town would know Abby was ordering men's clothing.

"I'm not sure I'll be able to make it this year. I have quite a bit of work to do," Abby said, ignoring Mrs. Patterson's inquisition.

Abby moved to pick up the boxes, but before she could, Clay grabbed them off the counter, reading the names on them. A dark flush colored his cheeks, and his eyes flashed with anger as he moved toward the door leaving Abby no choice but to follow.

Abby unlocked the door to her truck and opened the extended cab portion so she could slide the packages into it. Clay didn't say anything until she was done.

"Who are you buying men's clothes for, Abby?" Clay demanded softly.

Abby frowned at Clay before answering. "That's really none of your business, Clay."

Clay grabbed Abby's arm as she moved to get into her truck. "I think it is. I've been asking you out for the past four years, and you will hardly give me the time of day. Who are you buying clothes for?"

Abby sighed. "Clay, I like you as a friend, nothing more. You should know that by now. Please, just leave it at that and find someone else."

"I don't want someone else, Abby. I want you. You live up on that damn mountain all alone. It's not safe. You should move into town." Clay moved closer to Abby, trapping her between his body and her truck seat. He twirled a long piece of her hair that had come loose between his fingers. "You know I'm attracted to you. Why won't you give me a chance?"

Abby swallowed hard. Clay had never come on to her quite this aggressively. Before, it was almost a teasing game between them, one Abby had never really taken seriously.

"Clay—" Abby began but was silenced as Clay wrapped his hand around her neck and pulled her into him, kissing her deeply.

Abby was so startled by the kiss she didn't even think to resist. Clay had never tried to kiss her before. Now he was not only kissing her, he was doing it in the middle of the parking lot of the post office. A soft cough behind them caused both of them to jump.

Abby looked over Clay's shoulder to see Mrs. Patterson grinning as she locked up the post office. Abby blushed. Now, everyone in Shelby and every county within a fifty-mile radius would know the Sheriff of Shelby got caught kissing in the parking lot. Abby felt like a teenager getting caught making out.

"I have to go," Abby muttered, pulling herself into the driver's seat of her truck. "I still have to get groceries."

Clay backed up with a grin on his face, tipping his hat to Abby as she pulled out of the parking lot. He had staked his claim on Ms. Abigail Tanner, and he knew Mrs. Patterson would help let everyone know it. Whistling, he walked over to his truck. Abby might not have said she would go out with him, but she had not resisted him when he kissed her. He was off tomorrow, so he might just make a trip up into the mountains.

Abby had forgotten all about the incident with Clay by the time she was winding her way back up her driveway. She was thinking about Zoran and his golden ship. She couldn't believe that, out of all the places in the world for an alien to land, it was in her own backyard. She wondered what her grandparents would have thought about him. Abby absently reached up and rubbed the gold around her neck. She could feel the thin gold chain warm under her touch. She knew the creature, or whatever it was, enjoyed it when she rubbed it. It would often try to wrap around her fingers, moving in and out. She was amazed at how fast she had gotten used to it. She wondered what it was like where Zoran and the gold creature came from.

As Abby rubbed the gold necklace around her neck, flashes of images poured into her mind. She saw huge trees and creatures that resembled dragons in Earth's mythology flying through the air, gold armor covering their bodies. She saw a city of white rising out of the dense forests surrounded by huge walls that towered high into the sky. Large crowds of men and women were strolling about what looked like a market with the gold creatures taking on all kinds of shapes and sizes. She saw what looked like spaceships flying over the city and landing, while others took off. She saw Zoran naked and surrounded by lots of females who were rubbing on him. The gold necklace around her neck seemed to realize it shouldn't have shown her that image, and it quickly faded away.

"Hey! No fair," Abby said, sucking in her breath as her heart beat wildly.

She didn't even realize she was stopped in the middle of the driveway until the last image faded. She felt a wave of pain around her heart at the sight of Zoran naked with so many females. Obviously, he didn't lack for female attention. She would be damned if she would be one of his harem girls! It wasn't like it was likely to happen anyway. After all, he wouldn't be here much longer. She got the impression his family was on their way to get him. It would be better for both of them if she kept a distance between them. The kiss they shared this morning wasn't a big deal. Hell, Clay had kissed her too, and it didn't mean anything to her. She would just have to make sure it didn't happen again—with either one of them.

Abby finished the drive up the mountain. Try as much as she could, the image of all those women rubbing on Zoran wouldn't fade from her mind. Abby bit her bottom lip as she prepared herself to face him. She wouldn't let him know she found him attractive. She would concentrate on her work. She found if she did that it helped. It helped when her grandmother died, and it helped when her grandfather passed on. It would save her from making a fool of herself now.

* * *

Zoran had been pacing back and forth on the front porch of the small cabin for the past hour. It was beginning to get dark and Abby still had not returned. He tried reaching out to her, but his symbiot refused to answer his call. He growled, scaring Bo who was playing with his tennis ball in the front yard. Bo immediately lay down and rolled over to be petted. Where was she? Why was it taking so long? Had something happened to her? He knew he should have gone with her. He should have insisted she take the weapon he tried to give her. What if she was hurt? He paled. What if she was being held captive, or worse, dead? He shuddered at the thought, calling out to his symbiot again almost frantically. He felt a wave of dizziness pass over him as it finally answered him. He growled, wanting to know why it hadn't replied before. Flashes of Abby driving down a road with the wind blowing through her hair flashed through his mind. He could hear her singing. His grin faded as he saw a man approaching Abby. The man appeared to be wearing some type of uniform. He couldn't hear the conversation between them but he could tell from the look the man was giving Abby that he desired her. A deep growl exploded out of his chest when he saw the man holding Abby and kissing her. Zoran felt a flash of fury as the man pulled away from Abby, smiling at her. She had not resisted the man. Jealousy burned though him at the thought of Abby in another's embrace. She was his!

Zoran's head jerked around as the lights from Abby's transport flooded the front of the cabin. Zoran growled again as he watched her pull up. The dragon inside him roared for him to claim her, to put his mark on her. Zoran was at the truck's door before Abby even turned the engine off.

Abby laughed as he pulled the door out of her hands. "Not in a hurry to help get the groceries out, are you? You know, most men run the opposite way when they know it's time to bring them in."

Zoran was so lost in the haze of jealousy he didn't hear what Abby said. He needed to know if the images his symbiot sent to him were true. Zoran pulled Abby from the seat of the truck and into his arms, holding her close while he breathed deeply of her scent. The scent of another man still clung to her. A deep growl erupted from the back of his throat as his hand reached up to hold Abby's jaw still as he sniffed her.

"What are you doing?" Abby asked, breathless.

She thought it funny Zoran would react so strangely to her returning with groceries. She thought he must not have figured out how to work the microwave or make a sandwich and was just hungry. But the possessive way he grabbed her and the way he was growling told her he was upset about something.

Zoran growled again when Abby tried to push him away, warning her not to resist. He could smell the other man on her skin. The thought of the other man's scent on his true mate was too much for the dragon in him. He had to put his own scent on her. Gripping her neck in his large hand, he brought his lips down on hers, crushing her in his arms as he tried to gain control of his jealousy.

Abby resisted at first. Fighting the possessive hold Zoran had on her. She didn't know what was wrong, but he was obviously upset about something, or he had missed her more than she had thought. Abby was just beginning to relax and respond to Zoran's kiss when the image of him naked with so many women rubbing on him flashed into her mind. Twisting her head to the side, she took a shaky breath before trying to push him away from her.

"What is your problem?" Abby demanded. "I haven't been gone all that long, and even if I had been, you have no right to manhandle me!"

Zoran pulled back glaring down at Abby. She was his. He was frustrated that he could not explain this to her. She had no right to allow another male to touch her. A Valdier male was very, very possessive of his true mate. He would not think twice about killing any male who even looked too long at his mate. For another male to touch her, mark her with his scent, was more than the dragon in him could bear. He wanted to kill the male. If Abby purposely tried to leave him for another, he would do whatever was necessary to stop her, even if it meant tying her up or locking her away until she realized she belonged to him. He would never let her go. In Abby's case, it was even more potent, because not only had *he* chosen her as his mate but so had his symbiot, and from the feel of it, his dragon. This was very rare. As the ruler of his people, he would be expected to produce many heirs, and only in a union where he, his dragon and his symbiot, accepted the female would this happen.

"*Mine*," Zoran growled as Abby tried to push him away.

"*Mine!*" Zoran roared, the dragon in him finally overcoming his control.

Abby's breath caught in a gasp as she watched Zoran's face change. His eyes glowed with molten gold and his pupil's became long narrow slits. As she watched, green, gold, and red scales began forming as his head began to shift into the form of his dragon. His hands began to elongate, turning into sharp claws. Abby heard the sound of tearing as his shirt split open, and long, leathery wings appeared out of his back. A sound penetrated Abby's brain as if from a distance. It sounded like a whimper. That was the last thing Abby remembered as everything faded to black.

Zoran was so upset over the other male's scent on his mate and Abby's apparent rejection of him that he was unable to control his dragon any longer. He felt the change as it swept over him, enjoying the feelings of power and freedom as he let his beast free. What he had not expected was Abby's fear at his transformation. He saw her flinch as he roared out and then the stunned panic as he began to shift. It was only when she collapsed unconscious in his arms that he realized just how much he had frightened her.

CHAPTER 7

Abby stretched her arms over her head, arching her back like a cat. She didn't feel nearly as tired as she had been. It was only when she felt her skin on the sheet that she froze. Something was wrong. She never, ever slept in the nude. She had tried it once and it felt too uncomfortable, not to mention she had gotten cold. Right now, though, she felt nice and warm, like someone had put a heating pad or an electric blanket on top of her.

Opening her eyes, Abby turned her head to look outside the window. Frowning, she rose up on her elbows. The sun was just coming up. She didn't remember getting ready for bed last night. Turning her head the other way, she let out a squeal of terror. She was not only in bed naked but she was in bed with a naked man. Abby tried to roll out of the bed but was pinned instead by the sheet tucked around her. She was warm was because her other side was pressed up against Zoran's hot, naked body.

"What are you doing?" Abby squeaked. She tried to drag the covers up to her chin.

"You have awoken," Zoran said with relief.

After Abby fainted last night, he had brought her inside. He undressed her and placed her in his bed, but she still did not wake up. As the long night passed, Zoran became concerned and had his symbiot constantly monitoring her to see if she was injured. He finished bringing in the food products, guessing what went where by the temperature of it, while he waited for her to recover. When she appeared to have fallen into a deeper sleep, he finally undressed and joined her in the bed, as was his rightful place as her mate. He held her throughout the night, waking frequently to make sure she was well.

Abby frowned. She really needed to learn his language or get one of those translator devices, because this one-way communication was getting on her nerves. Abby's eyes widened as she recalled her last thought before everything turned black. She stared at Zoran, picturing how his eyes and face had changed.

She remembered his skin turning to scales and wings coming out of his back. He had turned into a dragon. A real, live dragon!

Making sure she had the sheet tucked up under her arms as she rolled over until she was propped up on her one elbow, Abby tentatively reached out to touch Zoran's face. It was warm and smooth. She moved her hand down to his shoulder, running her hand gently over his back where the wings had been.

"You changed. Last night, you changed into a dragon. I saw you," Abby whispered, her eyes wide with awe.

"*Zi*," Zoran said hoarsely.

Abby sat up pulling the covers with her. "Can you do it again? Change?" She asked.

Zoran frowned. He did not want to frighten Abby again. He liked having her in his arms. He liked her touching him. He did not like the look of terror on her face as she stared at him last night before she fainted.

"*Ni,*" Zoran said, shaking his head firmly.

"No? No, you can't change or no you won't?" Abby asked staring at Zoran.

Zoran ran his hand through his hair frustrated. He wanted to explain why he wouldn't change but there was no way to do so where she could understand. He had six more days before his brothers arrived and could have a translator implanted into Abby so they could communicate. This was driving him crazy. There was so much he wanted to ask her, so much he wanted to tell her and yet he couldn't. Swinging his long legs over the side of the bed, Zoran stood up completely at ease with his nudity. It wasn't until he heard a gasp and turned to see Abby pulling the covers over her head that he began to chuckle then laugh. She was so adorable with her shyness. It had taken all of his enormous will power the night before not to take her after he undressed her. If not for the fact that he wanted to watch her respond to him, he might have considered taking her anyway just so he could mark her as his. As it was, he had barely been able to cover her up without touching her. During the night, she had gotten cold and sought the warmth of his body. He was only too willing to offer his body to hers. It was pure hell as the scent and feel of her in his arms made sleep impossible. Now, he stood before her harder than hell and she was shaking like a leaf under the covers of the bed they had shared.

Abby kept her eyes firmly closed as she stuck her head out from under the covers. "Laugh all you want to, but I don't normally have naked men in my bed. Now, go into the bathroom so I can get out of here."

Zoran growled at the idea of Abby having another naked man in her bed. The sound made Abby's eyes fly open as her gaze flew to his. He had made that same sound the night before right before he changed into a dragon.

Zoran moved back to the bed, pulling Abby up into his arms. He moved so fast that Abby hadn't even seen him. The sheet was ripped out of her hands as he pulled her close, crushing her lips to his as he kissed her deeply. Abby could feel the coarse hair on his chest rubbing against her breasts. Zoran groaned as he moved one hand behind Abby's head to hold her still while his other hand moved down over her body to rest on her bare hip; never before had Abby been held so intimately against a man. A shiver of desire ran though her as her pussy clenched with desire. Zoran pulled back, sniffing. He let out a growl when Abby tried to pull away from him. He could smell her desire. It was a heady scent, and he breathed it in deeply. Moving his hand down from her hip until it covered her moist mound, he refused to let her look away from him or move as he let his fingers brush the hot pubic curls.

Abby couldn't help the gasp that escaped her. She had never felt so hot or needy in her life. She struggled to break Zoran's hold, but she couldn't look away from him as he slid two fingers into her pussy. Abby's hips jerked at the invasion of her body. She moaned as he rubbed her clit before pushing even deeper into her. Abby shook as she felt the hot desire build inside of her. Instead of letting her go, Zoran lowered Abby until she was lying flat on her back in the huge bed. He still kept his grip on her neck and never took his eyes from her, even as he lowered his head to catch one of her nipples between his lips.

Abby jerked, arching upward as Zoran grasped her swollen nipple between his lips. A cry escaped her as her hips jerked in response to the pleasure she felt; the move drove Zoran's fingers deeper into her hot channel. Zoran sucked deeply on her nipple before releasing it. He never took his eyes off of Abby's as he moved to her other nipple. Abby couldn't contain her moan of need as he moved over it, his hot breath causing the nipple to swell, almost painfully, in expectation. Abby's hips were moving back and forth on their own, driving Zoran's fingers deeper and deeper each time as her body picked up the age-old rhythm of lovemaking.

"Please," Abby whimpered. She didn't know what she was begging for exactly, just that she needed relief from the pressure building inside of her. "Zoran, please."

Zoran moved down to replace his fingers with his mouth. He needed a taste of Abby. Her scent had been driving him insane since he woke up yesterday morning. He needed her like he needed air to breathe. Abby cried out as his mouth covered her mound, pushing closer to him. Zoran moaned at Abby's response to him. Using his tongue, he ran the rough edge over her clit, causing Abby to scream as pleasure swamped her. Zoran gripped Abby's hips holding her to him as he sucked, licked, and drank her essence, burning it into his soul. Abby cried out loudly as her orgasm took hold of her. Zoran moved up between her legs settling his thick, heavy cock against her vagina. Lifting Abby's legs until her knees bent over his forearms he pushed slowly into her.

"Mine, *elila*. I claim you as my true mate. No other may have you. I will live to protect you. You are my mine," Zoran said in his language binding them together as he drove forward into Abby's slick entrance.

Abby cried out in shock as Zoran pushed through the thin barrier of her virginity. She gasped several times as pain washed over her. Zoran roared as he realized Abby had never been with another. He forced himself to hold still for a moment to let Abby adjust to his thickness and size. She was his, totally. She had never belonged to another. The dragon in him wanted to roar out a challenge to any man who would try to take her from him now. He would kill anyone who tried to harm her. His hips began to move on their own accord. He pulled out almost all the way before pushing back into Abby's body as deep as he could go. Abby's gasp of pain and shock quickly turned to moans of pleasure as Zoran began pumping into her faster and harder. His arms and neck strained as he fought his own release until Abby could again felt the hot release of pleasure he wanted her to have. Reaching down between them, he flicked her sensitive clit with his finger driving her over the edge. The muscles in Zoran's neck stood out as he roared his release for all to hear. Abby watched in disbelief as Zoran threw back his head, his eyes closed, and his mouth falling open as he filled her with his hot seed. Never had she seen anything so beautiful or so erotic. Her own body responded to Zoran's claim on her, clamping down on him as if claiming him for herself.

Zoran held still until he felt the last of his seed empty deep inside of Abby. His scent was now deep inside her, claiming her as belonging to him, Zoran Reykill, leader of the Valdier. She was now his queen and would always belong only to him. Her body would never accept another male. Zoran collapsed on top of Abby, holding himself up by his elbows so he wouldn't crush her under his huge body. He ran little kisses over Abby's forehead and cheeks before rolling over and holding her tightly against his body.

"You are mine, *elila*," Zoran murmured softly as he ran his hands possessively over Abby's soft figure.

Abby sighed contently. She couldn't undo what had happened. She had always been honest with herself. She really didn't understand what happened but she would accept the reality of it. She wanted Zoran from the first moment she saw him lying unconscious in the damp meadow of her mountain. She knew she would not have very long with him. What lay between them was an impossible fantasy as they literally came from two different worlds. In as little as a few days, he would be leaving to return to his world, and she would remain on hers. She believed in fate. He was meant to crash on her mountain, and she was meant to find him. What happened next would take care of itself. The only thing she regretted was they would not have very long to be together. He couldn't stay here with her; it would be too dangerous in the long run and she couldn't leave; this was her world, her home.

Abby pressed a kiss into Zoran's shoulder before turning to roll out of the bed. It was a little pointless being shy now about her body, especially after what Zoran had just done to her. She stood next to the bed, looking down at Zoran with a soft smile, before walking toward her bedroom. She needed a few minutes alone to deal with what she had just done. She pressed a hand to her stomach as she thought of the consequences of her actions. She wasn't worried about getting pregnant. The likelihood of their two species being compatible enough to reproduce was probably slim to none. No, what she was worried about was losing something far more important. She worried she would lose her heart to the one man she could never have. She knew she loved him. She didn't know how she knew. She hardly knew the man but she could feel it deep down inside her. Stepping into the shower, Abby tilted her head back letting the warm water wash her tears away.

CHAPTER 8

A smile curved Zoran's lips as he watched Abby fix a meal to break their morning fast. He was concerned when she left the bedroom without a word. Deep down, he knew she needed time alone to come to terms with what had happened. He knew she did not understand everything that had passed between them; he could tell by the small sad smile she gave him. She thought they would only have a few days together. There was no way to tell her it would be much, much longer. He had no regrets for what passed between them. He accepted that she belonged to him and had no regrets or qualms at the thought of taking her away from her home. She would have to adjust. He would be there for her, guiding her as she made adapted to his world.

They ate in a comfortable silence. Zoran helped dry the dishes after breakfast. He watched as Abby gazed out the window, her eyes distant for a moment before she seemed to remember he was there with her.

"I have to work today. If you want, I can show you where I'll be, then you can do whatever you want. I have a project I've been working on and it is almost done. I would like to have it finished by today or tomorrow at the latest. Edna will be home the day after tomorrow to get Bo and Gloria. I promised to show it to her before I delivered it to my clients," Abby said softly, staring out the window instead of looking at Zoran.

Zoran was concerned by the distant sound in Abby's voice. Ever since she had got out of the shower, she seemed to have withdrawn into a world of her own. He walked over to her and tilted her head back until she was forced to look at him. His breath caught at the deep sadness he saw there. He leaned over and gently kissed her. He wrapped his arms around her holding her tightly against his body while he ran his hand up and down her back trying to give her comfort and reassurance.

Abby felt her body relax as Zoran held her. She wouldn't let the depression of knowing their time was short ruin what time she did have. With a determined smile, Abby tilted her head back and gave Zoran a light kiss before pulling out of his arms. She grabbed his hand and motioned for him to follow her.

Abby called out for Bo to follow as she led Zoran down the path to her workshop. She unlocked the double doors pushing them open so the light breeze could float through it.

Zoran stood still as he took in all the different colors as they flowed through the bright interior. Delicate flowers, bowls, birds, and other creatures, including dragons were hanging, sitting, and spinning on delicate mobiles from every corner of the huge building. In the center was a magnificent piece standing almost three feet high. The beautiful sculpture was encased in clear glass; inside were small creatures with wings fluttering around delicate, brightly colored and intricately designed flowers. As Zoran moved closer to the centerpiece, he could see what appeared to be tiny dragons floating in thin air.

He had never seen anything so beautiful. He looked at Abby as she tied a large cloth around her slim waist. He watched for the next two hours as Abby heated different color glass in a huge furnace and moved it around, blowing and turning it over a smaller flame until more flowers appeared. Her slim fingers, twisting and turning as she moved, turned a molten liquid into flowers and tiny creatures. When she had a dozen little flowers, she moved to the glass-enclosed case, moving the figures inside a tiny opening and heating them until they stayed where she wanted them. He liked listening to her sing as she worked. She didn't even seem to realize she was doing it or that he was even there as she became totally absorbed in her work.

Zoran was surprised when Abby began talking after being quiet for a while.

"I've been working on this piece for over six months now. I started it right after my grandfather died," Abby began softly. "My grandmother and grandfather raised me after my mom decided raising a baby was too much effort." Abby sighed. "I guess that isn't right. My mom was young and had gotten in with the wrong crowd. My grandparents were very well-to-do in Los Angeles and thought moving here might help her. It didn't. She had me when she was still a child herself. At least she recognized that and left me with my grandparents when I was a month old. My mom died from a drug overdose when I was two."

Abby paused as she attached another flower. Glancing up at Zoran, she saw he was watching her intently as she talked, so she continued. "I had the best childhood any child could have. I had a whole mountain as a playground and two wonderful people who loved me very much. There was always music and laughter in the house. My grandmother started doing blown glass as a hobby to help her deal with the loss of my mom. Soon, my grandfather was doing it and between the two of them they started making money off of it. I was doing it by the time I could walk. Now I enjoy being able to do it and make a comfortable living from it. I consider it a gift from my grandparents."

Abby turned as she heated a rod to close the small opening. She finished the piece at last. She would take pictures of it before she went up to the house and email it to her clients. She would need to schedule when they wanted it delivered. They said they would send their private jet to Shelby's small airport so she could personally deliver it. Maybe she would need the time away to get her feelings under control. If she was lucky, she thought sadly, maybe Zoran would be gone before she returned. She didn't know how she was going to have the strength to say goodbye to him without making a fool of herself.

"I'm finally done with this piece. If you have some things you would like to do, I can finish up here. I just need to take some pictures for my client and clean up. I can meet you up at the cabin later. I don't think you've been to see Goldie yet," Abby said with a teasing smile.

"Goldie?" Zoran frowned as he watched Abby shut down the furnace and start to pick up the scraps of glass on the worktable.

Abby laughed as she held up her wrist and gently rubbed the gold band. "Goldie!"

Zoran chuckled as he walked down the path. He was going to check on his ship and check in with his brothers. He wanted to tell them he had mated. He knew they would be surprised. None of them thought they would ever settle down with just one woman. He especially never thought to do so. He could imagine their surprise. He never thought to name his symbiot, either. It would have been like naming himself. That Abby affectionately called it 'Goldie' made him laugh.

* * *

When he got to the meadow and entered his ship, he went immediately to the communications panel and opened a connection. A solid screen formed and within moments, Kelan could be seen. Zoran sat down on the chair that formed under him. All around the interior, gold waves coursed along the walls as the energy contained within the symbiot moved.

"Kelan, how are things?" Zoran asked as he stared at his brother.

"Well. Creon has information you will be interested in. He wants to meet with you as soon as we return. We are ahead of schedule and should be there as much as a day earlier. Trelon and his symbiot have been playing with the engines again," Kelan said with a grin.

Trelon and his symbiot were always messing with something. His brother could never leave anything alone. He took a deep breath. He was reluctant to break the news of his mating to his brothers separately. He would rather tell them once he could introduce Abby to them. He didn't know why he felt the need to wait, he just did. He wanted them to like and accept Abby for the beautiful woman she was. He talked to Kelan for another hour before breaking off. He realized he missed Abby. He would finish preparing his symbiot for departure before he went to her. He couldn't shake the feeling of fear that she would hate him after he did what he was planning.

* * *

Abby finished cleaning the workshop, took the needed pictures, emailed them from her cell phone, and prepared the packing material. She received a text stating a plane would arrive for her early the day after tomorrow after she explained she couldn't leave before then. Edna was due back tomorrow and she needed to be there for Edna, Bo, and Gloria. Abby sent a confirmation. She had a feeling Zoran wasn't going to be happy with her but realized she had no choice. She promised she would deliver and set the piece up. It was part of the price and she had already been paid. She still had her responsibilities and her reputation to maintain.

There was still plenty of light left, and Abby knew she could always use the firewood so she decided to cut up the tree that had fallen by the barn. Abby was in the middle of chopping it when the sound of a truck pulling up out front caused her to stop. Abby walked around to the front thinking that maybe Edna had made it back sooner than she expected only to stop with a groan when she saw Clay climbing out of his Sheriff's truck. This was the last thing she needed right now, she thought with dismay.

"Hey Clay, what brings you up to the mountains?" Abby asked, setting the ax down to lean against the door to the barn. She moved toward the cabin, taking off her gloves and wiping her hands on her jeans as she went.

"You beautiful!" Clay said as he walked over and pulled Abby into his arms pressing a kiss to her surprised lips.

"Clay!" Abby flushed. She had never known him to be so aggressive before. "Seriously. Let me go."

Clay laughed as he held Abby close to his body. "Abby, I've tried being patient. A man can only wait so long, you know."

Abby felt a flush of unease fill her at his words. "Clay, I thought you understood. I like you but I don't feel that way about you. I…"

Clay laid a finger against Abby's lips. "Shush, all I'm asking is for a chance, Abby."

Abby shook her head sadly. She knew she could never love him. Tears filled her eyes; she didn't like hurting anyone or anything, and she knew she was about to hurt Clay.

"Clay, I can't give you false hope. I like you as a friend, nothing more," Abby said softly.

Clay looked down into Abby's eyes. His face tightened in anger. He had spent the last four years trying to get Abby to notice him, to give him a chance, and she wouldn't even try.

"Is there someone else?" Clay demanded angrily.

Abby tried to pull away, but Clay tightened his arms around her, refusing to let her go. "Yes."

"Who is he? How long?" Clay demanded hoarsely.

"You don't know him. I just met him a few days ago," Abby said, trying not to hurt Clay any more than she had too.

"That's bullshit, Abby. A few days ago? Shit, you haven't been off this mountain in over a week until yesterday! How could you have just met him if you haven't left this damn mountain?" Clay asked roughly.

Abby frowned. "How could you know the last time I left the mountain? For that matter, how can you know every time I come into town and know exactly where I am?"

"I know everything about you, Abby. For the past four years I've tracked every move you've made. I know when you go to a gallery showing and who you talk too, who you call, when you leave your mountain, everything, baby," Clay said softly.

Abby felt a chill go down her spine. Clay had been in the Marine's Special Ops before he was hired four years ago as Sheriff of Shelby. She didn't know much more except that he had been discharged after his last tour. She figured it was just time for him to get out.

"Clay, please let go of me. You're scaring me," Abby said as she tried to get her hands between them.

"You don't have to be afraid of me, baby. I just want to protect you. I love you, Abby. I've loved you since the first time I saw you," Clay said as he brushed a kiss along her forehead.

Abby began to struggle a little, stopping only when Clay grabbed her hair tightly in one fist. He brushed a kiss over her lips. "It will be good between us, Abby. You'll see. You won't remember anyone else but me."

Abby shivered as Clay continued kissing her. She couldn't move her head because of the grip he had on her hair. He held her close to his body with one of her legs between his and bent slightly back so she couldn't knee him without falling first. She cried out in pain as he jerked her head to one side pressing a biting kiss to her neck. She fought the urge to gag when he ran his tongue up her neck and along her jaw. Surely Zoran would come soon. If she could get to the gold bands on her wrists maybe she could somehow call him. He seemed to be able to communicate with them. As if the symbiot could tell Abby needed help, the ones on her wrists moved up her arms.

Clay let out a yell when he felt a shock go through him. Jerking back away from Abby, he stared down at her in disbelief as he shook out his arms.

"What the hell was that?" Clay demanded, furious.

"Clay, you need to leave. Right now. I apologize if you think I've been leading you on but I never tried to. I told you over and over I wasn't interested. If you know what is good for you, you'll leave right now," Abby said moving back toward the cabin. If she could get away from him she would be okay.

"What. The. Hell. Was. That," Clay said through clinched teeth.

"It's a new personal protection device I picked up in New York," Abby lied. "Like you said, it can sometimes be dangerous living alone in the mountains. Now, please leave."

Clay took a step toward Abby just as Bo burst out of the path leading to the meadow barking excitedly. He glanced at Bo for a moment before backing toward his truck. He looked at Abby one more time before he slammed the door shut.

"It's not over, Abby. You are mine and I keep what is mine," Clay said as he put the truck into drive and pulled out spinning gravel as he went.

Abby sank to the ground shaking so badly she couldn't stand any longer. She had never been so scared in her life. How could Clay know every move she made? She shivered as she realized what could have happened if she hadn't been wearing the gold bands or if Bo hadn't come back to her. Abby fought tears as she tried to understand what Clay had told her. She no longer felt safe—and the bad part was she couldn't call the local authorities.

* * *

Zoran gave Abby as much space as he could before his need to touch her overwhelmed him. Moving down the path, he watched as Bo took off at a run. He had grown attached to the little fur ball. He found it amusing how Bo never went anywhere without the odd little green ball in his mouth. Zoran had just reached the beginning of the path when the symbiot on Abby sent a sharp warning out to him. Zoran froze as the breath was knocked out of him. He reached out, feeling Abby's fear. He sensed the presence of another male near her. Letting out a loud roar, he fought to keep his body from shifting, but the dragon sensed a danger to his mate and burst forth. He felt the shift of his dragon come over him as he burst down the path leaping into the air. In moments, he was soaring high above the trees. He flew over Abby's cabin, his sharp eyesight seeing her sitting on the ground with her arms around Bo. Turning his head, he looked around him for the danger he sensed. His gaze locked onto a transport similar to Abby's moving at a high rate of speed down the winding road. He flew ahead further down the road where he landed and moved into the shadows of the trees. He wanted to see what had scared his mate and determine how much danger there was from the male. He watched as the transport slowed to make a turn. His eyes narrowed in on the man behind the wheel of the transport. Breathing in deeply, he drew the man's scent into his body.

He would never forget the scent, and if the man ever came near Abby again he would know. He let a low growl roll out as he recognized it as the man who kissed Abby yesterday when she went to town. He breathed a stream of dragon fire, curving it through the air straight toward the truck. The almost translucent symbol of a dragon appeared on the hood of the truck. The man had been marked. If he came close to Abby, Zoran would kill him.

Zoran turned, shifting back into his dragon form, as he moved back into the shadows. With a quick sweep of his powerful wings, he flew straight up into the air until he reached the path between the meadow and the cabin. Feelings of self-doubt filled him. What if Abby's fear was of him discovering her with another man, not of the man himself? A bright flame of anger and jealousy flared inside him. It would not matter. He had claimed her. He had marked her with his scent. Jealousy turned his vision red at the thought of Abby wanting to be with another male. Zoran leaped up to the porch, throwing the door open as he fought his own fear of losing her.

Abby jumped when the door of the cabin swung back so hard it bounced off the doorframe. Zoran stood in the door outlined by the late afternoon light. Abby frantically wiped at the tears she couldn't seem to stop. She was shaking so bad she felt like she was going to shatter.

Zoran stood for a moment taking in Abby's tear-stained cheeks and her pale complexion. She looked so delicate, so fragile, so vulnerable. When she raised a shaking hand to wipe away the tears, Zoran's heart melted. He could smell her fear. Breathing deeply, Zoran's eyes glittered a dark gold as he smelled the man's scent on her.

"Oh, Zoran," Abby whispered moving toward him. She wrapped her arms around him, afraid her shaking legs would give out at any moment. "I was so scared."

Zoran held Abby tightly as she buried her face in his chest, sobbing out her fear. Zoran gently picked Abby up in his arms. He shut the door with one foot and moved toward the bedroom. He sat on the edge of the bed holding Abby tightly while he rocked her back and forth until she stopped shaking.

"Tell me," Zoran said frustrated.

Abby wasn't sure what Zoran just said, but she guessed he wanted to know what happened. She owed him that considering she had just soaked his brand new shirt. Laying her head on his chest, she let out a shaky breath before she began.

"Four years ago, a man named Clay Butler moved to Shelby. He was a decorated soldier and considered a hero. The people of Shelby elected him as Sheriff. A sheriff is our local law enforcement. They are there to protect people. Not long after he started, he began following me around whenever I went to town. I thought it was kind of funny. He is a good ten to twelve years older than I am but it wasn't only that. I just wasn't interested. He didn't push it too much when my granddad was with me, but he was a little more aggressive when I was alone, so I didn't go often without gramps. Anyway, about six months ago, right after my grandfather died, he started pursuing me a little more aggressively. I never encouraged him. I told him I wasn't interested but he always seemed to know when I left the mountain. He would show up at the post office when I did, or the grocery store, or the hardware store. It didn't matter. He would be there. I just thought it was strange that he always knew where and when I was there. Yesterday, when I went to town, he showed up at the post office. I could tell he was mad when Mrs. Patterson mentioned I had received some men's clothing in the mail. He asked me who they were for and I told him it was none of his business. He took the packages off the counter before I could. I didn't want to make a fuss in front of Mrs. Patterson." Abby looked at Zoran with red-rimmed eyes. "She's the biggest gossip in town."

Zoran pulled Abby's head back down to his chest. He could feel the rage beginning to build as he thought of what she was about to say. "Clay asked me again when we were outside who I was buying the clothes for. Before I could say anything, he grabbed me and kissed me. Mrs. Patterson came out of the post office and caught him. He just grinned like it was natural for him to be kissing me. I told him again to leave me alone."

Abby rubbed her face in Zoran's chest, drawing in a deep breath before she continued. "He pulled up a little while ago. He grabbed me and wouldn't let me go. He told me he loves me. He said he knows every move I make, who I talk to, who I meet. He said I was his. He said he keeps what is his. I told him to leave, that I had met someone else."

Abby drew in a shuddering breath, fighting back a sob. How had her life gotten so screwed up so fast? She tried to keep a low profile. She didn't go asking for trouble. She just wanted to be left alone.

Zoran's dragon was going mad with the scent of the other male on his mate. He needed to give her reassurance and make her feel safe, but if he didn't get the other male's scent off her soon, he was going to scare the hell out of her when he marked her. He wanted to find the male and kill him. He still might do that before they left. But first, he needed Abby to know he would never let anything happen to her.

CHAPTER 9

Zoran held Abby close to him before he gently pushed her back far enough to begin unbuttoning her blouse. Abby drew in a startled breath when she felt Zoran's fingers on her blouse. Soon he was pushing it off her shoulders, letting it drop down on the floor by the bed.

Abby arched toward him, letting out her breath as Zoran ran his lips along her neck, "What are you doing?"

Zoran groaned. He wouldn't lie to her, even if she couldn't understand what he was saying, "My dragon cannot stand the scent of the other male on you. If I don't bathe you and make love to you, he will claim you." He released the clasp on Abby's bra drawing a deep breath as her breasts were freed.

Zoran gently cupped them in his hands. "Beautiful," he whispered as he bent his head to lick a nipple with his rough tongue.

Abby shuddered. "Oh God that feels so good."

Abby began fumbling with the buttons on Zoran's shirt, trying frantically to pull it off of him. She wanted to feel his skin against hers. She needed him so much she could hardly wait. She leaned forward, running small kisses along his throat before biting his neck near his shoulder.

Zoran felt the startled growl of his dragon at the challenge. "Abby, *elila*, my dragon is too close. If you are not careful, you will incite him."

"I wonder if your dragon wants me the same way?" Abby breathed not realizing she was mirroring Zoran's own concern as she moved to stand in front of him. She could see how his eyes had changed. Narrow slits of black looked back at her through the dark gold. "I saw him this morning, when you made love to me. Does he want me, too?"

Abby suddenly felt wild and wanton. She wanted to make love with Zoran. She wanted him to claim her. To make her know she belonged to him and no other male could ever take her. She wanted to see his dragon in him as he made love to her. She wanted them both. She moved to stand slightly away from him. She unzipped her pants and pushed them down. She kicked her tennis shoes off and finally stood nude in front of Zoran. She cupped her breasts and rubbed her nipples, feeling them swell to tight peaks.

"What does your dragon want, Zoran? I can see him looking at me through your eyes," Abby asked huskily as she pulled her hair loose from the pony tail so that it fell in waves down her back. "What do you want?"

Zoran felt his dragon roar at what Abby was asking. She was asking his dragon what he wanted, acknowledging him as a part of Zoran. His dragon wanted to catch her, to mark her, to claim her as his. Zoran knew Abby had no idea what she was doing. He tried to speak, to let her know, but his dragon would not let him. Zoran stood up. He quickly removed his clothes, daring Abby to turn and run. He barely had control of himself and his dragon. If she ran, he knew he would lose all control. A small part of him wanted her to run, wanted to see if she could handle what he and his dragon could do to her, another part was afraid it would be too much for her. That it would break her.

Few Valdier females could accept a relationship that included a male, his symbiot, and his dragon. That was why the number of true dragon shifters being born had decreased over the past few hundred years. Most females could barely accept the need to share themselves with the male and his symbiot. For most females, if a male tried to let his dragon mate at the same time as he did, the female could actually die. Most females could not handle the dragon's fire or the desire that flooded her body during mating, burning at her to mate frantically until both the male and the dragon were sated. He didn't want to chance Abby going through the fire, but his dragon was demanding he do so. If she was his true mate, it roared, she would be able to handle both of them.

Abby looked over her shoulder at Zoran, "If your dragon wants a piece of me, he has to catch me first," Abby said with a mischievous smile, right before she bolted for the bathroom.

Zoran felt his dragon's response to the challenge. Within moments, his eyes shifted even further, and he felt the dragon fire build in his throat. A low growl escaped before he leaped forward after Abby. Abby turned and squealed with delight. She had finally made Zoran lose a little of that hard control he always seemed to have. She loved it when his eyes changed. She watched as they had changed earlier that morning, when he had made love to her for the first time. She also saw the colors of his dragon's scales ripple under his skin when he came. She had never seen anything so wild, beautiful, and hot in her life. She felt his hot breath on her neck right before she felt his hands grip her from behind. She looked down and saw as his hands shifted back and forth between his hands and the claws of his dragon. Abby shivered with desire as she thought of belonging to both of them.

Turning, she pulled Zoran's head down to hers, kissing him deeply as her hands roamed his body. She was on fire inside. She needed to feel him take her. She needed him buried deep inside her. Reaching behind her, she turned on the shower. When she felt the steam rising behind her, she pulled back far enough for Zoran to see her wiggle her finger at him in invitation.

"Come into my lair," Abby whispered, as she reached out and grabbed Zoran's hand pulling him toward her.

Zoran's eyes narrowed as she talked directly to his dragon. He felt his skin ripple with scales as Abby challenged his dragon to please her. Zoran swung his head back and forth as he caught the scent of the other male still clinging to Abby's skin. As he moved slowly toward her, his eyes narrowed on her neck. He moved so fast Abby didn't even see him move, until he pinned her to the wall of the shower, one hand on her throat and the other on her ass. Pulling her up and pressing her back against the wall of the shower, Zoran leaned forward to peer at Abby's neck where Clay had bitten her. The sight of another male's mark on Abby infuriated him. His vision turned red as a killing rage filled him at the thought that another male had the nerve to mark his mate. Zoran let his head fall back, and a loud, unearthly roar left him as he called out a challenge to the male.

Abby stayed perfectly still, watching Zoran's dragon react to the mark Clay had left. She could see his anger at the bruising on her neck reflected in his eyes. She knew Zoran and his dragon would never hurt her. She could feel Zoran shake as his dragon fought back the rage. She lifted her hands to his face, cupping it between her palms.

"Mark me. Take his mark from me. Make me yours, completely," Abby whispered softly, staring up into Zoran's elongated eyes. She tilted her head back exposing her neck.

Zoran felt his body shudder at Abby's words. She was asking him to mark her as his for all to see. To mark like this would mean everyone would know she had accepted both him and his dragon. It would also change her in a way she had no way of knowing. If she survived the change, they would be as one.

Zoran felt the dragon fire burning deep even as he tried to hold it back. It was too dangerous. She was not as strong as the females of his world. Her body could never survive the change. Even as he thought it, he felt the fire burning him, fighting to get out. Without conscious thought, he bent forward, letting his teeth shift to sharp points as he bit down on the mark on Abby's neck breathing dragon fire as he did.

Abby felt a sharp pain that quickly turned to fire as desire flooded her. She cried out at the intensity of it. Unable to stand still, she pulled Zoran's head down holding it to her neck as he continued to breathe dragon fire into her. She could feel the fire moving through her, as she pressed closer to Zoran.

"Please, I need more," Abby whimpered trying to get closer to Zoran. "Please, Zoran."

Zoran cupped Abby's ass, pulling her up until she could wrap her legs around his waist while he continued to breathe dragon fire directly into her blood stream. He was unbelievably hard. He had never before had the combined desires of both his dragon and his own body to deal with. When he felt the fire finally begin to burn down, he pulled back far enough to capture Abby's mouth with his own. He could feel the heat burning in her body. For the next several hours, it would get hotter and hotter. If she survived, he would have much to teach her. If she didn't, they would both perish, for his dragon could not survive without her now.

Zoran groaned as he buried his hot, throbbing cock into Abby in one thrust. He needed her. Pushing through her tight vagina, while holding her against the wall of the shower, he pounded into her desperately. Waves of hot desire began flowing through Abby as the dragon fire spread. Abby cried out, arching against him as she came. Zoran shouted as he followed her a moment later. He remained holding her shoulders against the wall while he pushed his cock deeper into her. His head was bowed as he tried to catch his breath. It had begun.

Abby ran her hands through his long black hair shivering as the water started to turn cold. "Zoran?"

Zoran jerked his head up, his eyes glowed a bright gold. "This is just the beginning, Abby. You wanted my dragon and you got him. You have both of us, and now you will know what you have asked of me." He knew

Abby couldn't understand him, but he also knew she could see what she had unleashed.

Abby's eyes widened in shock, she could see his dragon clearly in his eyes. She could see the desire of both of them for her, their need to claim her, mark her, and make her theirs. She nodded as Zoran lowered her to the floor. She shivered as a wave of desire rushed through her as her body answered the call.

Zoran turned the shower off, his back to Abby as he tried to hold back. "Abby, go to the bedroom. Or better yet, run. I'm not sure how long I can hold back," Zoran begged desperately.

Abby watched as Zoran's body shuddered as he fought for control. "I'll be waiting for you in the bedroom." Abby ran her hand across Zoran's back, scraping her nails across the scales rippling in waves.

Zoran let a moan escape at the feel of her nails. "Too late."

Zoran swung around, picked Abby up, strode into the bedroom, and tossed her on the bed. With a growl, he was on her, pulling her thighs apart as he bent and buried his head between them. Abby screamed as Zoran covered her mound. She felt the fire of his dragon as it brushed a breath across her sensitive clit. When she moved to get away, hard hands held her still, gripping her thighs and pushing them even farther apart. Abby whimpered as she felt a long rough tongue stroke her. When Zoran pushed his finger deep inside her, she couldn't contain the cry of pleasure that escaped her as she pushed down on it. Abby felt her climax as it exploded out of her, leaving her screaming, as she felt Zoran lapping and sucking her until she sobbed. She was shaking so badly, she was afraid she would break apart.

As soon as he lapped up her cream, Zoran pulled away and picked Abby up and turned her over until she lay on her stomach. Pulling her up by her hips, he mounted her from behind in one hard stroke. He pushed in as deep as he could go and still tried to go deeper, only stopping when he heard Abby whimper in protest. He pulled out and pushed in hard. He could not take her gently. He was burning with the need to make sure all traces of the other male were gone. He pushed in again, and then pulled back, watching as his cock disappear into her again and again. When he felt the dragon fire building inside Abby again, he increased his speed wanting to bring her pleasure as she rode the hot wave of transformation.

Abby whimpered, feeling the fire building inside her again. She felt like she was going to burst into flames, the desire building so hard and fast inside her she wanted to scream. Throwing her head back, she let out a loud scream as the wave of fire hit her hard and fast, throwing her into another orgasm. She could feel her body clamping down around Zoran as she came, pulsing around his cock, as if she were trying to bury him even deeper inside her. She pushed back needing more of him as it crested again and again in hot waves. She began crying as it increased.

"More...Oh God, I need more," Abby cried, shivering as the fire burned even hotter inside her.

Zoran clenched his eyes tight as he felt Abby fist his cock deep inside her. He could feel the heat building even hotter. His body reacted in an age-old primal desire to satisfy his mate. Never had he felt the waves of desire so intense or his need to fulfill them so strong. He pumped into her again and again, both of them climaxing as the dragon's heat engulfed them both.

The heat had been driving them for the past few hours, allowing both of them only a short rest before the fire began again. Zoran worried about Abby. He knew she was exhausted, but each wave only seemed to get hotter. Zoran watched as the transformation took a hold of Abby. She was unaware as the first faint ripples of dragon scales, pale blues, golds, and whites, began forming under her skin. Mounting her from behind, Zoran watched as thin membranes fanned out along her back. His dragon roared in triumph at watching his mate being born.

Holding Abby by the hips, he knew the next wave would be even hotter, and he wondered if she would be able to handle his total possession of her. She had no experience with the ways of his people or of a dragon's heat. He would take her over and over throughout the night until the fire either burned out or burned her to death.

Abby collapsed on the bed breathing heavily. Zoran pulled out of her, rolling her over and sitting on her. Grabbing her nipples between his fingers, he pulled and pinched them getting her ready for the next wave. He shoved his cock toward her mouth.

"Take me," he growled, pushing his cock against her lips, daring her to take him in every way.

Abby's eyes flashed with fire as she met Zoran's challenge, daring her to take him in her mouth as he had her pussy. She could taste herself on him as she let him slide his long cock into her mouth. He pulled her nipples, enjoying how she moaned around him as he pinched them tightly. Zoran rocked his hips back and forth sliding deeper and deeper with each thrust. He let go of one of Abby's nipples long enough to stroke her throat.

"*Zi*, Abby. *Zi!*" Zoran groaned as he felt his climax build. He knew he didn't have long before the last wave of heat would hit Abby. He shouted out, "*Zi!*" as his climax hit him hard and he watched as Abby drank his hot seed. He rocked his hips squeezing her nipples, forcing her to drink all of it before he pulled out and kissed her deeply wanting to taste both him and her on her lips.

"Zoran." Abby looked up at Zoran with tears in her eyes. She loved him so much she felt like she was going to die when he left. She didn't want to lose him. Reaching up, Abby kissed him deeply as she felt the fire building again. Panting, she pulled away as the fire burned her from the inside out. Screaming at the intensity of it, she arched up as it moved through her. She could feel hot juice flood her pussy as the wave moved over her. Crying out, she shook from the hot desire burning her.

Zoran pulled Abby's thighs apart and again buried himself in her, pushing deep. He could feel the heat. This was it. He prayed she was strong enough to handle what he was about to do. Pushing into her over and over, he waited for the right moment. When he felt his dragon roar, he pulled out, turning Abby over and pulling her up onto her hands and knees. He had no way of preparing her for this, no way of warning her about what to expect. He could only hope she would accept him. He pushed into her pussy again, pumping her as he spread the cheeks of her ass. Using her own juices, he slid two of his fingers deep into her pussy while he pumped her, ignoring her whimpers at the tight feeling. Pulling his fingers out, Zoran slid them up to the tight ring of her ass, wetting it before pushing past it. Abby jerked, groaning at the burning. Zoran held her tightly with one arm around her waist. Murmuring words of comfort, he tried to stretch her, to prepare her for his thick, long cock. He would take her hard and fast. He would possess her totally, marking her with the mark of his dragon as they both came. He needed to wait until she was at the peak of her transformation. He pushed his cock deep into her pussy waiting until the telltale heat built to its hottest. He tried to prepare her as best he could. When he felt the heat build and Abby's whimpering increase to cries and pants, he pulled out of her pussy and against her tight anal ring. Grabbing her hips to prevent her from pulling away, he slowly pushed past the barrier, ignoring her cries as he settled all the way in.

"Now, *elila*. Now, come for me," Zoran groaned as he began moving.

Abby pushed back trying to get away from the burning. She was on fire. As Zoran began moving, she felt the heat inside her build to a boiling point. Screaming, she became a wild thing. Fighting as the wave of desire crested over and over, she clawed the sheets as she pushed back trying to take as much of Zoran as she could, anything to put out the fire of desire burning through her. She felt her orgasm building and building, but it wouldn't come. She was crying and pleading with Zoran to help her, to give her the release she needed, to put out the fire burning her. She needed him.

Zoran waited until he couldn't hold on any longer; he leaned over Abby and pulled her up against his chest, burying his cock as far as it would go, pinching her nipples, and sinking his teeth into her neck completing his marking. Abby screamed so loud and so long she finally lost consciousness as her orgasm hit in wave after wave. Even as Zoran pulled out of her exhausted body he could feel the aftermath of her climax as it continued to rock her. Zoran stumbled as he stood. Never before had he or his dragon ever been totally sated. He felt weak at having finally found one who could satisfy him completely. He took a deep breath before picking up Abby. He would bathe her and let her sleep for a little while. It would give her body time to finish the transformation.

Zoran's hand shook as he gently brushed Abby's hair away from her damp forehead. She had survived. His true mate had survived and she had accepted him, his dragon, and his symbiot. Even as he thought that, he could feel the gold symbiot moving around Abby checking to make sure she was okay. He gently bathed Abby in the big tub in the bathroom, enjoying being able to hold her as she slept. As he stared down into her flushed face, he realized he loved her. He loved her gentle, compassionate nature, her sense of humor, her love for other creatures, her acceptance of him and who and what he was, and her ability to create beautiful works of art. He loved everything about her. He felt a pain around the region of his heart at the thought of anything ever harming her. Holding her close, he knew he would never let her go.

CHAPTER 10

Abby blew a wisp of hair out of her face. She was glaring at Zoran and he was glaring at her. They had been at the staring contest for the past thirty minutes, ever since Abby told Zoran she was going away for a day, possibly two.

"Zoran, I have to go. I have a contract. My clients have already paid me a great deal of money. I'll be back as soon as I can, but I have to go. I have no choice."

Zoran ran both of his hands through his long hair. *"Ni! Ni! Ni!"*

He would not let her out of his sight. What if something happened to her? What if she didn't come back? It was too much. He couldn't let her go. He growled in frustration. How could he explain that he and his dragon could not be away from her? Not even for a few hours! Well, maybe for a few hours, but dammit, he didn't want to be away from her.

He glared at her. Why did she have to be so stubborn? What did it matter if she didn't go? She wasn't going to be on this planet much longer anyway if he had his way, and he planned on having it. He had never been so frustrated at not being able to communicate in his life. He had known her a total of three days, five if he counted the time he was unconscious, which he didn't, and he had never been more frustrated in his life. He paced back and forth before grabbing Abby and pulling her out the door. He couldn't wait any longer. He had to get his brothers to help him.

Abby struggled to keep up with Zoran. She knew he was frustrated, but so was she. She had never had sex until yesterday morning and they made up for all the years since she hit puberty in one night! She was still a little sore, though the symbiot seemed determined to help her overcome that. She had never been as embarrassed as when she caught one of the little gold devils moving around her private parts this morning. When she screamed, she had to put up with Zoran laughing at her as she tried to get the thing to move back to her wrist. Zoran then proceeded to make love to her over and over, just so he could hold her down and watch as his symbiot healed her. It wouldn't have been so bad but it seemed the more they did *it*, the more she wanted *it*. She was becoming addicted to sex!

As they approached the meadow, Abby pulled back. She had touched and caressed the golden ship but she had never been inside it. She didn't know what she expected but she wasn't sure she wanted to be inside anything that was alive. Zoran threw her a frustrated look before turning and picking her up into his arms. Abby just pressed her lips together. He wasn't the only one frustrated. The only time they seemed to really understand each other was when they were in bed, and then all they did was grunt, groan, moan, and scream, a very universal language Abby decided.

Zoran sat down in a chair, turned, and gave a command. Suddenly, a view screen appeared with several males on the other side. Abby couldn't help but be fascinated as she sat up in Zoran's lap. They were all tall, dark, and handsome. Zoran spoke rapidly to the man on the screen who turned and spoke to another man before turning back to stare at Abby.

"Wow. This makes the Chip-n-Dales look like boy scouts," Abby said, breathing shallowly as she stared at the men who were staring at her with the same look of astonishment.

"Who is Chip-n-Dale?" Zoran asked.

"Mm, exotic male dancers. I saw them at a club in New York that one of my clients took me to once," Abby replied absentmindedly, more focused on the view screen.

It took a minute for her to realize she actually understood Zoran. Abby turned in his lap, her face lighting up. "I understood you!" She threw her arms around his neck, laughing as she pressed little kisses all over his mouth.

"Ah, Zoran. Who is the female and is she taken?" Kelan asked from the bridge of his ship.

Kelan was stunned to hear from Zoran again so soon. He was even more astonished at his request for an open translator to be patched into their com. When he saw the female, he felt a deep reaction to her. She was truly beautiful. That she was sitting on his brother's lap had been a surprise. That she was beautiful had not. His brother had a way of attracting beautiful women wherever he went.

Abby giggled. "Are you offering?" she teased back. She was almost giddy at finally being able to understand Zoran.

Zoran growled deeply, "Yes, she is taken. She is my mate, and no," he said to Abby, "he is not offering." Zoran pulled Abby into his arms possessively.

Abby laughed, pressing a kiss to his neck. "How did you do this? I can understand you? Is it only when we are here?"

Zoran ran his hand down Abby's arm possessively. "Yes. Soon, you will be able to understand me. My brothers should be here day after tomorrow. They will bring you a translator."

Abby pulled away, looking at Zoran in dismay. "The day after tomorrow!" she said in horror. She only had today left to be with him. She was leaving for New York tomorrow morning and probably wouldn't be able to be back before he left.

Abby tried to pull away from Zoran. She didn't want to see the look of pity she knew must be on the faces of the men on the space ship. She was sure she looked like a lovesick puppy dog.

"Yes. This is why you cannot leave," Zoran said pulling her against him.

"I have to go. My client is sending a plane for me in the morning. I told you that. Edna will be back today to get Bo and Gloria. I leave tomorrow and, if I'm lucky, I can get a flight back and be home late tomorrow night or early Sunday," Abby said, feeling sick to her stomach. She was not ready to say goodbye to him.

"You don't have to leave so soon, do you? Couldn't you wait a few more days?" Abby asked desperately. Glancing at the man standing on the view screen, she turned back to Zoran. "I mean, it's not like they haven't traveled a gazillion light years for you. What could a couple more days make?"

Zoran's eyes grew dark as he tried to hold his temper. "Abby, you do not understand. You are my mate. I forbid you to go."

"You forbid?" Abby looked at Zoran in amazement. "Who died and made you king? I'll go if I want to. I made this commitment before I met you, and I plan on honoring it. I keep my promises and commitments."

"What about your commitment to me?" Zoran said, furious. "And my father died and made me king!"

"Commitment? We never made a commitment to each other. I knew you wouldn't be here for very long, but I thought I would have at least a few more days to be with you before you left. I understand you want to return to your home. I would, if I was in your place. And, what do you mean your dad died and made you king?" Abby responded hotly.

"We did make a commitment. I marked you! My dragon marked you! My symbiot claimed you as my true mate," Zoran said through gritted teeth. "My father was king of the Valdier and now I am."

"I didn't know what that meant, so it doesn't count. I can't have a long-distance relationship with you. How is that going to work with you god knows where and me here on my mountain? I really don't think my cell phone plan covers those types of calls. And what do you mean, you're a king?" Abby asked confused.

A light cough came from behind them and they turned in unison to look at the man staring back and forth between the two of them in a combination of amusement and confusion.

"Zoran, haven't you been able to communicate with your...I'm afraid I did not get your name, my lady?" Kelan asked.

"Oh dear, I'm so sorry. My name is Abigail Tanner, but everyone calls me Abby. It's a pleasure to meet you..." Abby said, pushing a strand of hair out of her eyes, as she looked shyly at Kelan.

"Kelan, my lady. Zoran's younger brother by three years," Kelan replied, enchanted by the beautiful, strong, stubborn female sitting on his brother's lap. He never thought to see a female who could stand up to his brother, especially when he was angry.

Abby smiled, showing off her dimples. Zoran groaned. He was powerless when Abby smiled with her dimples. He knew his brother would be a total pushover.

"It's a pleasure to meet you, Kelan. I will be happy to welcome you to my home when you arrive," Abby said softly.

Kelan stared at the delicate beauty. "It will indeed be a pleasure to meet you, Lady Abby, and I look forward to enjoying your hospitality."

Abby turned to look at Zoran. "See, he doesn't mind if you have to stay an extra day. Please say you will, Zoran. I promised and I could never live with myself if I didn't keep it." Abby gave Zoran her sad puppy dog eyes and pushed her lower lip out just a little. It always worked with her grandfather.

Abby heard Kelan groan. "Zoran, let her finish her duty. We will wait for her return."

Zoran moaned. He had a feeling he was better off when she couldn't understand him. He seemed to get his way more.

* * *

Zoran growled again as he listened to Abby talk to Kelan, then Trelon, then half a dozen other men on his brother's crew who came to see the lovely alien female who wore the dragon's mark on her neck. Abby was still unaware of it. When they finally made it into the bathroom this morning they were more interested in each other. By the time they got out of the shower, the mirror was fogged to the point neither of them could see a reflection. Zoran was too distracted to explain to Abby what had happened. Every time he got close to her, he couldn't seem to keep his hands and mouth off of her. They even made love on the path up to his ship. Abby was so beautiful bent over the limb of a branch with him mounting her from behind. Bo quickly lost interest and took off for the meadow without them. By the time they got to the meadow, he took her again, this time on the soft grass. It seemed his dragon was making up for lost time.

Trelon gave him the idea of using his symbiot to make a connection with his ship which would have an open line to their translator. The symbiot on Abby would allow her to understand what Zoran was saying. It was a round-about way for them to communicate, but it was better than nothing. They spent the rest of the afternoon talking about a little bit of everything. Abby discovered that Zoran and his brothers often got into trouble when they were younger for all types of misadventures. His mother was still alive and doing well though she preferred to spend most of her time at their mountain home away from the city. Zoran did not really have a favorite color because he had never really thought about it, while Abby loved blue and green. He was a definite meat eater and could not understand why Abby did not eat meat at all. They ended up having a heated discussion on that.

Abby was determined to enjoy being with Zoran to the fullest. She didn't want to think about his leaving in just a few days. She knew she loved him. She also knew she would never love another man. Picking up her grandfa-ther's guitar, she sat on the swing watching as Zoran played with Bo. It was funny watching him. She could almost picture him playing with their chil-dren, a dog of their own running around, while she sat on the porch swing watching them. Tears burned her eyes at the dream that would never come true. Strumming the strings, she began playing and singing some of the country songs her grandmother had written. She loved playing and singing. It helped her, especially when she was feeling so emotional.

Zoran threw the green tennis ball for Bo before turning to watch Abby. She was wearing a tank top and a pair of jeans. She left her hair down after the last time he stole her hair band and it fell in waves around her. She had kicked off her shoes and sat with one leg tucked under her as she used the toes of her other foot to gently push the swing back and forth. She had reached over a few minutes before and picked up an odd shaped instrument, which she was absently strumming on. Now, she began playing a beautiful song about a young girl who was in love. Her husky voice echoed over the mountain. Zoran thought it was the most beautiful sight he had ever seen or heard before.

Abby seemed totally unaware of how captivating she was. Love for her swelled through him to the point of pain. He not only desired her physically but he desired being around her, listening to her, watching her as she did little things, like making them a meal or talking to the animals, stroking and petting them to offer them love and comfort. Her gentleness wrapped itself around his heart.

Zoran walked slowly toward the porch where Abby sat playing and singing. She smiled as he came up the steps. Bo followed him, panting, before dropping the ball and lying down next to him.

"My grandparents and I used to sit on the porch every night the weather allowed. We'd sing and play together for hours. If it was cold, we would sit in the living room in front of the fireplace and sing. My grandparents and my mother are buried on this mountain. I knew I would never leave it. This is my home, where I was always meant to be." Abby smiled sadly at Zoran.

"There are mountains where I come from. They are just as beautiful as these," Zoran replied softly, his gold eyes darkening with emotion. "I would like to show you the mountains of my home."

Abby shook her head, fighting back tears. "Tell me about them," she said huskily. "Let me see them through your eyes."

"Close your eyes," Zoran said, moving to sit next to Abby. He reached over pulling her onto his lap, his arms tightly wrapped around her. "I want to show you them the way I see them."

Abby lay back against Zoran enjoying the feel of his strong arms. Closing her eyes, she relaxed, as he began telling her about his home, his mountains.

"During the early morning, a dense fog covers the lower mountains. The trees on our mountains are much larger than the ones you have here. Some of the branches are as big around as the trunks of your trees. They have to be to support the weight of the dragons who love to fly through them," Zoran began.

Abby gasped as the symbiot around her neck wove with the one around his. The warm gold bands intertwined together, sending her pictures of what Zoran was describing. She watched as he shifted to his full dragon form, a powerful green, gold, and red dragon. He wasn't massive like the dragons from the movies; he was the same height as he was now if she didn't count his tail and wings. She saw his gold symbiot form armor over his body, a gold breastplate, head armor, and armor for his claws, wings, and tail. She watched as his powerful wings swept up and down, lifting him straight up into the air in a matter of seconds. She turned her head. It was as if she could almost feel the wind blowing across her face as he flew through the thick fog, swerving in and out between the huge branches of the trees before breaking through the cloud cover to soar over the mountain ridges. Abby set the guitar down without opening her eyes so she could spread her arms out as if she was the one flying. Zoran's voice rolled over her, through her, as if they had become one and the same. She felt the freedom and power of the dragon in flight. She laughed as she felt the spray from the waterfall as he dove, swirling, in and out of the rainbow-colored mist. She looked at his reflection as he skimmed the water; his back claws drew faint ripples as they barely touched the surface before sweeping back up. She could feel his love for his home and the freedom of being who he was in those few precious minutes. Her breath caught in her throat as she felt him landing on one of those thick branches so he could look down upon the world he called home. It was incredibly beautiful.

The sound of a truck coming up the drive and Bo barking drew them out of the world they had escaped to. As the gold around their necks separated, they gazed at each other unable to bear ending the journey they had just traveled together. Zoran leaned forward and brushed his lips gently across Abby's lips.

The sound of a truck door slamming finally broke through the Abby's daze. Turning to look at their visitor, a smile broke through at the sight of Edna's worried look. Abby pulled herself reluctantly out of Zoran's arms and off his lap to stand up.

"Welcome home, Edna," Abby said smiling at her old friend.

"Hello, dear. I hope I'm not interrupting anything," Edna said with a small smile and a knowing look.

"Zoran, I'd like you to meet an old family friend. Edna knew my grandparents when they lived in Los Angeles and has known me my whole life. She's my god-mother," Abby said, walking forward to wrap her arm around Edna's waist. "Edna, this is Zoran. He needed a place to stay for a few days."

Edna frowned. "Just for a few?"

She looked back and forth between Abby and Zoran. Abby blushed, unable to meet Edna's knowing look. Zoran immediately liked the older woman.

"It is a pleasure to meet you, Lady Edna," Zoran said.

Edna frowned. "What did he just say? The only thing I halfway understood was my name."

"He said it was a pleasure to meet you. Zoran isn't from around here," Abby said, pushing her hair behind her ear as she looked nervously at Zoran. She had never, ever lied to Edna and knew she could trust her with her life, but she wasn't sure she could trust her with Zoran's.

"Where are you from, young man?" Edna asked in her usual point blank I-want-a-straight-answer-right-now voice.

Zoran looked amused. He could tell Edna was very protective of Abby, and he appreciated that. He also thought it was funny she called him a young man. While he did not know the age limit of Abby's species, his could live for thousands of years. His father had perished in a tragic accident during a hunt; even so, he was over a thousand years old. His mother would have perished, as well, if she had been his father's true mate, but his symbiot or his dragon never fully accepted her. They still reproduced but that was mostly because his mother came from a long and distinguished line of dragons. Theirs was a union of two strong clans bound together to form one strong one.

"A very distant land," Zoran replied, looking directly into Edna's eyes.

"He's from a very long way away, Edna. Would you like some coffee or tea? I also need to show you the piece I finished. I'm flying out tomorrow morning to New York to deliver it. Can you believe they are sending their private jet for me?" Abby said, moving up the steps giving Zoran a warning look as she passed him.

Edna chuckled. "I'd better skip tonight. I love my kids, but damn if they don't tire me out. I want to see this piece you've been hiding from me and get Gloria and Bo back home before it gets dark, if I can."

Abby chuckled as she slipped her shoes on. The three of them walked down to Abby's workshop. Edna was impressed with Abby's latest masterpiece. Edna told Zoran about how proud she was of Abby and how special she was. Zoran just grinned as he watched Abby blushing and trying to get Edna to hush up. Zoran was unable to stop himself from grabbing Abby during one of her blushes and kissing her—deeply—right in front of Edna who stood there grinning.

"Zoran..." Abby protested huskily. She could feel the fire burning inside her. Whenever he touched her she seemed to ignite into flames.

Edna laughed. "I don't think you two will mind if I call it a night. Zoran, can you give me a hand getting the trailer hooked up and getting Gloria loaded? Abby, I know you need to get your piece packed for transport. I'll send Zoran back down to help you when I'm done with him."

Abby took the hint. *Abby stay, Zoran go.* Edna wanted him alone for a few minutes. Abby gave Edna a kiss and a hug telling her she would see her later in the week when she went into town. Edna hugged Abby tightly. She had a feeling it might be the last time she saw her precious little girl. She fought back tears at the thought. She didn't know why she felt that way, she just did.

Brushing Abby's hair back, Edna gave Abby one last kiss on her forehead before looking her deeply in the eyes, "You know I love you, baby girl. I'm glad you finally found the man to complete you. Be happy."

Abby fought back tears. "I love you too, Edna."

Abby stood by the door for a few minutes watching as Edna and Zoran walked back up the path toward the cabin. Taking a deep breath, she turned and began the tedious task of packing her creation.

* * *

Edna waited until they were far enough away from the workshop so Abby wouldn't hear what she had to say. She was determined for Abby to find happiness, even if it meant her moving far away. She couldn't put her finger on it, but she knew people. It had been her job for over thirty years in the entertainment business to know how to read people, and Zoran was like no person she had ever met.

"Who are you?" Edna turned looking at Zoran. "And don't try to bullshit me. I know people and you are not like anyone I have ever met. I need to know you aren't going to hurt Abby. I'd kill you myself right now if I thought you would. I just need to know my baby girl is going to be happy."

Zoran stood for a moment looking at the old woman standing in front of him. Looking down at the determination in the woman's face, Zoran knew he could not hurt her or Abby by taking Abby away without the woman knowing Abby would be all right. Staring up at the path to the meadow, he made the decision to let Abby's friend know just how much Abby would be loved and cared for. Reaching down, he took Edna's withered hand in his and nodded.

Edna was nervous as Zoran led her up the path to the meadow. She had been to the meadow hundreds, hell, maybe even thousands of times, over the thirty-plus years she had known Abby's grandparents. Bo ran ahead of them, used to the direction they were going now. Edna was beginning to grow concerned, until she stepped into the meadow and saw a large golden ship appearing out of thin air. She trembled as Zoran led her inside. He waited patiently for his symbiot to accept her as a friend of Abby's.

Turning to look at Edna, Zoran said softly, "I am Zoran Reykill, High King and Leader of the Valdier."

Edna's shaky hand went to her throat as she slowly sank down onto a seat that formed for her. "Oh, dear. You really aren't like any man I've ever met before, are you?"

Zoran smiled gently, "I highly doubt it."

"How...?" Edna began. "How did you meet Abby?"

Zoran's lips curved into a soft smile. "She found me. I was captured by another species. I was injured and landed here looking for a safe place to heal. Bo actually found me. Abby took me into her home and cared for me and my ship," Zoran said, waving his hand to the golden ship they sat in.

Edna looked around at the inside of the spaceship in awe. The walls sparkled and moved as if they were alive. She could see the colors swirling around them. The chair she was sitting on formed out of a type of liquid metal, fitting itself to her. She noticed that once the huge man in front of her sat down, additional panels of gold formed in front of the seat he was in. It looked almost like a monitor of a computer only paper thin. Edna shook her head. It was more than her old mind could absorb all at once.

"You're going to take her away, aren't you?" Edna whispered, her eyes filling with tears. "When you leave, you plan to take her."

"Yes," Zoran said firmly. "She is my true mate. I have marked her as mine and neither of us can be with another."

"She doesn't know, does she?" Edna asked sadly. While her heart broke for her own loss, she couldn't help but be happy for Abby.

"No. She thinks to stay here," Zoran said.

"What if she doesn't want to go? Surely, she has the right to know, to make the decision..." Edna began. Her voice faded as Zoran shook his head.

"We can't be apart. To do so would mean death for us both," Zoran said. "Edna, you need not worry. I will do everything in my power to make her happy. I love Abby very much. She is my other half."

Edna smiled through her tears, nodding. "I believe you. She is very special. She deserves to be happy. Just keep her safe and love her. That's all I could ever ask."

Zoran leaned forward and gently cupped Edna's cheek. "I will, I promise."

Zoran watched as Edna drove slowly down the drive, Bo's head hanging out the window with the green tennis ball held tightly in his mouth. He turned and walked down the path to Abby's workshop. Tomorrow, two of his brothers would be here. Unknown to Abby, he would not be staying any longer than it took for her to return to him. Then, he would never let her go again.

CHAPTER 11

Abby bit her lip as she drove down the highway trying not to start crying again. Zoran had been very reluctant to let her go. After he came back to the workshop last night, he helped her finish packing her creation. It took both of them to get it into her truck. She hoped whoever came to pick her up wouldn't mind helping her load it on the jet. Afterwards, they walked back to the cabin where Abby fixed them a light meal. After dinner, they sat outside talking about Abby's clients and how far New York was from California. Zoran hadn't said anything but Abby could tell he wasn't pleased. Unable to deal with his disapproval of her leaving, she kissed him, the fire of desire burning in her blood. They spent most of the night making love before Abby fell into an exhausted sleep not long before daybreak.

Breakfast was a quiet affair. Abby finally noticed the mark on her neck in the shape of a dragon but didn't say anything to Zoran. Even now as she drove down the highway, she lightly traced the pattern with her fingers. It looked like a combination of a tattoo and a birthmark. All she cared about was it was a piece of Zoran. It marked her as his and his dragon and no one could ever take that away from her.

Abby pulled into the airport parking lot. The terminal was just a single, one-story building not much bigger than her workshop. Mrs. Patterson's husband, Harry, was the lone airport personnel, and he did that as a volunteer. He was a retired Air Force pilot and traffic controller. Abby liked the way he used to come up to the mountain to talk with her grandfather, especially after her grandmother died.

"Morning Abby, I just got a call that your ride will be landing in the next fifteen minutes. Need any help with your crate?" Harry said gruffly.

Abby smiled. "Morning Harry. If you don't mind holding the hand truck steady while I slide it down, I would appreciate it. I have this thing packed so tight I could probably air drop it down the Boswells' chimney and it would be fine."

Harry laughed in response. They spent the next twenty minutes talking about different things while they waited for the jet to finish taxiing. Abby was surprised when two women climbed down from the jet.

"Good morning. I'm Trisha Grove, and this is my co-pilot, Ariel Hamm. We are to assist you in any way you need and escort you to the Boswells' home in New York."

Abby looked at the two young women. Both were dressed in black form-fitting uniforms that flattered their figures. She had never seen a plane like the one they were flying. The jet had a slick design, and Abby could tell it was made for speed.

"Hi. I'm Abby Tanner. Thank you for coming all this way to get me. I can't believe the Boswells are flying me all the way to New York just to deliver this."

Ariel laughed. "They spare no expense, plus this is a write off. This is a new design for business jets and we get to test it. Both of us were Air Force test pilots, so this is one of the perks of the job. The jet is very safe and handles like a dream. They just wanted to test fuel efficiency and speed cross-country. We were happy to volunteer for the trip."

Harry's eyes lit up when Ariel mentioned their Air Force connection. A half hour later, both women were promising to give Harry an update on their flight when they returned Abby early the next day. The Boswells planned a reception for Abby's new creation and wanted her to stay the night for their dinner party. Abby was reluctant but knew it would be pointless to protest since the Boswells' connection could mean more contracts for work.

* * *

The flight to New York was uneventful. They made a brief stop in Nevada to refuel, since Shelby didn't have the jet fuel they needed. After their brief stop, Abby leaned back in her seat staring down at the passing landscape. She already missed Zoran so much she hurt. She could feel her dragon mark burning as if it were protesting her being so far from him. She absentmindedly rubbed it gently with her fingers. Leaning her head back, she smiled down at the two gold symbiotics on her wrists. They were weaving into different designs like they were trying to make her feel better. They both turned into the shape of a dog chasing each other. Abby giggled as she watched them running around her lap. Her eyes widened with wonder as both suddenly took the shape of little dragons and began flying around. She watched as they chased and played with each other for almost an hour before settling back down onto her wrists with a warm, contented feeling. She raised each one to her mouth, gently pressing a kiss on them.

Abby fought back tears at the idea of them leaving her when Zoran left tomorrow. She knew they couldn't survive without being near him and the mother symbiot. She felt a single tear track down her face at the thought of losing him. She didn't know if she would survive it. Closing her eyes, she drifted off to sleep as exhaustion swept through her.

* * *

Zoran paced back and forth in frustration. He was going out of his mind without Abby near. It took every ounce of willpower he had to let her go this morning. His dragon roared and clawed at him in fury. He had to get out of the cabin. Her presence and scent were everywhere. The sheets still held the scent of their lovemaking, making him ache to hold her. He strode up the path to the meadow and his ship. Maybe if he focused on what was happening back home and with the plans to attack the Curizans he would be able to take his mind off of Abby for a little while.

He ran his hand over his golden ship murmuring soothing words as he walked inside. The ship shuddered at the knowledge it would soon be able to transform into another shape soon. It missed the freedom of Valdier.

"Soon, my friend, soon you will be able to roam free," Zoran said as he sat down. Calling up the view screen, he turned to his brother, Trelon.

"Trelon, how goes it?" Zoran asked grimly.

"Well, we are within orbit of the planet. There are a number of satellites we have to redirect so their signals do not recognize anything out of the ordinary. The inhabitants of this world clutter their air space with a lot of junk. It is almost amusing to see how primitive they are. It is as bad as being on the hunt planet without the city complex," Trelon said with a glimmer of amusement on his face. He loved anything to do with old space junk. He collected it just to take it apart and see what it was used for.

"I've been monitoring their communications. They have many entertaining programs. Did you know there was a group of people shipwrecked on an island? And this yellow thing lives on the bottom of their ocean and cooks on a grill. How can a grill work under the water?" Trelon continued looking puzzled.

Zoran gave Trelon a frustrated look. "Have you heard from Creon recently?"

"He is being very secretive, but you know Creon, he is always that way. He doesn't want to say anything until we join him back home," Trelon replied. He hesitated before continuing. "Zoran, can I ask you something personal?"

Zoran looked up distracted. He was trying to reach out to the symbiot on Abby, but she was too far away. "Yes."

"Is it true you were able to complete the mating? I mean, a true mate, with the female from this planet?" Trelon asked quietly, for once totally serious.

Zoran sighed. He knew many would be interested in his mating with Abby. The sign of the dragon's mark on her neck would show she had mated with both him and his dragon. The sight of his symbiot on her would show she was totally accepted as his true mate. This was something all males craved, as it meant total satisfaction on both a physical and mental level. He had found his other half; he was finally whole.

"Yes. I have found my true mate. Abby not only accepted my symbiot but me and my dragon," Zoran replied.

"Is it true what they say, about the dragon's heat? That it is truly an incredible experience to finally be sated?" Trelon asked tentatively.

Zoran's eyes flashed for a moment before he realized his brother was not asking for details, he just wanted to know if everything they had ever heard as they grew up about the dragon's heat was true. That for once, the constant ache, the constant hunger was finally sated. The nagging discomfort was something they all accepted they would always feel until their deaths.

"Yes. While I ache and hunger for Abby, it is not the same. I miss her on a physical and mental level. Something I have never felt before. But the steady ache and hunger that clawed at my insides is no longer there. Only with her do I feel complete," Zoran said, looking at his brother with tears in his eyes. "I love her, Trelon, both as a man and as a dragon."

Trelon smiled sadly. "I am happy for you, Brother. I can only hope one day the rest of us can find a true mate like yours."

They spent the next several hours talking about life back home. The other diplomats were furious over Zoran's capture and had voted on an embargo of Curizan until the forces responsible for his capture were brought to justice. The city complex on the hunt planet also received a warning that such an event would not be tolerated, and it would be fined for not maintaining security as it promised. A new commander of the city complex was installed, and a full investigation was underway to find out what happened.

* * *

Abby sighed with relief as the last guest for the evening left. The Boswells did everything big. There had to have been over a hundred guests, all incredibly rich. Her piece was placed in the Boswells' private gallery, and Abby received numerous compliments, a few a little more personal than she liked, and a couple of promising prospects for additional work. She didn't push anything, since she was just too sad and tired to do so. All she wanted to do was get back on the plane and head back to California. Unfortunately, it would be early tomorrow morning before she could leave. Mr. Boswell explained they were waiting for a mechanic to show up from one of their facilities to accompany the flight back. Some of his managers wanted to have the pilots test a few things, and the mechanic was supposed to test the engine afterwards. There would also be another passenger, but Mr. Boswell didn't say more than that. Abby really didn't care as long as they left as soon as possible. She missed Zoran, and tomorrow might be her last day with him.

CHAPTER 12

Abby let out her breath in relief. They took off later than planned due to a weather front moving through the center of the country. It was dark as they neared the little airport in Shelby. The weather here was clear, and Abby could see the stars glittering out the window of the small jet. Their mysterious passenger spent most of the time with a sleeping mask on in the back of the plane. Abby never got a good look since the woman was already on the plane when Abby boarded. She talked quietly on a cell phone until they began taxiing for takeoff, then she slipped the sleeping mask on and Abby didn't hear a sound out of her again. The mechanic who sat next to Abby snoring softly turned out to be the total opposite. The mechanic turned out to be a little thing. The woman, which surprised Abby, had to be about five-foot-two and probably weighed a hundred pounds wet. She had a head full of dark auburn hair with streaks of purple in it. She had a scattering of freckles across her nose and a ready smile. She was perky while sipping one of the largest cups of coffee Abby had ever seen. As the woman talked up a storm and checked every nut and bolt on the plane, three times, Abby decided the woman shouldn't ever drink coffee or any other beverage with caffeine in it. She was like a bouncy ball let loose in the small space. She finally crashed about two hours before after saying she hadn't slept in over seventy-two hours. Even in her sleep she seemed to be working as her fingers moved back and forth like she was taking something apart.

The symbiot on Abby fell in love with the woman as she talked and petted them. Abby didn't know how on earth the woman seemed to know about them but she had taken one look at them and talked to them as if she did it every day. They behaved themselves, staying quiet while on Abby but Abby knew they wanted to play. Once the woman fell asleep, they turned into little birds and flew over to her, flittering around her face as she blew out little puffs of air.

Abby's pulse quickened as Trisha's voice came over the intercom to ask that everyone buckle up for landing. Cara Truman stretched out her arms and legs, shooting the little gold symbiot on Abby's wrists a wink as she sat all the way up.

"So, how long before we land?" Cara asked looking out the window. "Cool, not a cloud in sight. Man, this is a little bitty place, isn't it? Looks like the town I grew up in."

Abby laughed in excitement. "Yes, it is small but its home."

"Looks like you have a reason to be back. Is he cute? Does he have a brother?" Cara asked mischievously.

"Yes, he is, and yes, he has four brothers," Abby replied distracted before she realized what she had just said.

Laughing, Cara stretched again. "Busted! Well, if they are cute point me in their direction. I'm always looking for a good time in a small town."

Abby couldn't help but laugh. Cara had the kind of personality that any-one couldn't help but fall in love with. She was a ball of energy. Even sitting still she moved around.

Cara saw Abby's amused smile and couldn't help the rueful grin that curved her lips. "I'm a little ADHD. I couldn't sit still if my life depended on it, and I only sleep about four hours a night if I'm lucky. Drives everyone nuts but I get a lot done. I have an IQ out the kazoo. Needless to say, most people and all men can't stand being around me for more than five minutes. Oh, but I do love to drive them crazy first."

Abby chuckled. "Well, you haven't driven me crazy, and I have thor-oughly enjoyed your company."

Ariel's voice came on to say they would be at the gate in just a few min-utes, thanking everyone for flying Hamm Air, the only airlines where pigs did fly. Abby and Cara looked at each other before bursting out laughing. Both Trisha and Ariel had a very dry sense of humor.

* * *

The airport was dark except for the few lights on some of the nearby hangers and the airport terminal. Harry had gone home hours before. Since it was so late, Abby didn't have the heart for the four women to head back across country. While she wasn't sure about what to do, her grandparents always stressed good manners as she was growing up. Abby bit her lip wondering how Zoran would feel about her bringing home some new friends for the night. She could always let them use her grandfather's truck to drive back the next morning and work with Edna on getting it back.

"It's really late for you to head out tonight. Would you like to stay at my place for the night? It's a little ways up the mountain but it's really beautiful. I have an extra bedroom if you don't mind doubling up and an oversize couch that makes a great bed." Abby looked nervously, wondering if the women would be offended.

"Sounds great to me!" Cara said stretching. "I'd go bonkers if I had to get back in that tin can tonight. I'd love to meet your man. You said he had some brothers? Any chance of meeting them between tonight and tomorrow morning? I love meeting new guys. I'm trying to break my record of driving them off. I think the longest any have put up with me was ten minutes."

Trisha and Ariel laughed. "Ah Cara, I think that Danny guy lasted twelve. What do you think, Ariel?"

"Oh, at least twelve maybe even thirteen minutes," Ariel added.

Cara laughed out loud. "You two are nuts. You were so drunk you can't even remember his name. It was Douglas. Not, Dougie."

The three women burst into laughter. "Oh yeah, good ole Dougie. How could we forget? Unlike some people we know, Ariel and I both need at least eight hours of sleep more than once a month to survive. We would love to take you up on both of your offers."

Abby frowned, "Both of my offers?"

"Yeah, bed and brothers." Cara, Ariel, and Trisha smirked.

"I appreciate the offer, but I think I'll skip. I had transportation delivered earlier. I think I'll head out, since I slept most of the trip," the mystery woman said quietly, from the back of the plane as she came up as if out of nowhere.

"But, Carmen..." Ariel began huskily.

"I'll call. I promise," Carmen said quietly cutting Ariel off. "I need more time."

Ariel looked at the woman with tears in her eyes. "Yes, but how much? It's been three years."

"Enough, Ariel. I said I'd call." The woman grabbed her backpack and took off across the tarmac.

Abby watched quietly. She could almost feel the woman's pain. Her symbiot must have felt it, because she could feel them moving restlessly around her neck and wrists. She gently reached under the sleeves of her jacket and rubbed them.

* * *

Zoran reached out again for Abby. He had been trying all day to connect with her through the symbiot. He just needed to know if she was all right, if she was on her way home. His brothers and two other men had transported down earlier that morning. He met them in the meadow. It was good to see them, but nothing would compare to when Abby returned safely to his side. He felt a warm glow as his symbiot responded to the call from Abby's. He felt a shiver run through him. She had returned.

"Zoran, all is well?" Trelon asked, noticing his brother's sudden stillness.

Zoran looked at Trelon as if coming out of a daze. "She has returned."

Kelan and Trelon grinned at their brother, noticing a difference in him already. Zoran was not the only one impatient for his mate's return; his dragon fairly roared with the desire to see her as well.

Zoran looked at both of his brothers with a grin. "Soon you will meet my true mate."

They laughed and teased Zoran and his dragon with all the things they wanted to do to keep him occupied so he couldn't be alone with his mate. Zoran growled playfully at his brothers, rough-housing with them as they walked back to the cabin. The other two men would take his mother ship back to the warship, where she could safely change form. He, Abby, and his brothers would use a transport beam to return. He ached to show Abby the wonders of his world. He was just commenting on that fact when he felt Abby reach for him.

Stopping, he frowned for a moment before looking at his two brothers. "Abby will not be returning alone. There are three females with her."

His two brothers looked at each other with a mischievous smile. "Perhaps she brings our true mates to us," Trelon teased. "I, for one, am not ready, but perhaps Kelan, Mandra, and Creon might appreciate having one. I still have much to taste before I settle for one female."

Kelan laughed, grabbing Trelon around the neck. "You believe yourself a bull dragon to satisfy so many females. It takes that many because none could ever put up with you for long."

Zoran laughed as he watched his brothers joking around. He had missed much and would not be so eager to leave his home world again, once the situation with the Curizans was dealt with. He was about to join in when he felt a shaft of intense pain and fear. His dragon roared and clawed as he felt the danger to his mate. Before he could say a word to his brothers, he had already shifted and was lifting off the ground in a loud roar. Within moments, both Kelan and Trelon shifted and followed him without question, their symbiot transforming to gold armor around the bodies of their dragons.

CHAPTER 13

"I'll go get my truck ready if you three want to grab your stuff," Abby said watching as the woman walked off into the darkness.

"Sounds great," Cara said moving toward the jet. "It won't take me but a minute."

"More like a second," Ariel said turning away with a sad grin.

"Give us about ten minutes to secure everything and we'll be along," Trisha said, shaking her head as she watched Cara disappear into the plane. "Some of us don't move at Mach ten."

Abby laughed as she carried her overnight bag toward the parking lot. She gave a small sigh when she felt Zoran's symbiot reach out to her sybioses. She felt his warmth and relief come through. She smiled, happy to be home. Moving around to the driver's side of the truck, she was just unlocking the door when she felt something behind her. She started to turn when she was pushed up against the side, her arms pinned. She let out a startled scream that quickly turned to a whimper when her arms were pulled painfully back behind her.

"Hush, Abby. I told you I always know where you were," Clay said in a harsh whisper near her ear. "I missed you, baby, even if it was for only one day. I don't like it when you leave."

Abby shivered. Clay's voice sounded different, scary. "Clay, what are you doing? You're scaring me."

Clay slid a pair of handcuffs onto Abby's wrists snapping it tight over the symbiot. "Don't try anything, Abby. I didn't like what you did the other day. I'm going to have to punish you for that."

Abby whimpered again as she felt him pull her head back by her hair. He looked at her neck in the soft glow of the parking lights. "What the hell is that? Who the hell put that mark on you?"

Abby cried out when he pulled her head back even further when she didn't answer him right away. "Zoran. Zoran put his mark on me. I belong to him," Abby whispered.

Clay let out a soft expletive. "Not any longer. You're mine. I've played your fucking game for four fucking years. You're mine, Abby, and when I get done with you, you'll know it."

Abby started to protest when she felt a sharp sting in her neck and everything went black.

"Hey, Abby. You okay?" Cara asked as she moved toward the truck. "Ariel and Trisha are on their way. It didn't take—" Cara's words died off as she saw Abby crumble against the man.

The man's head jerked up when he heard Cara call out. Pulling a gun from behind him, he aimed it at Cara and pulled the trigger. Cara was already hitting the pavement when a soft pop went off. Within moments, the man picked Abby up and slung her over his shoulder, letting off another round of gunfire as he moved. Cara was rolling toward a golf cart parked nearby. She jumped, startled, when she felt a hand on her arm and let out a small scream.

"Shush. It's me, Carmen," Carmen said kneeling next to Cara. She looked up when she saw Ariel and Trisha running toward them.

"Shit, what happened?" Trisha said.

"Some asshole waylaid Abby. From the little I was able to gather, he isn't too happy she didn't choose him instead of this Zoran guy. He stuck her with something and has her cuffed. I'm going to follow him. Keep your line open; I might need some backup," Carmen said before running toward a motorcycle hidden in the dark between two hangers.

"We need wheels," Ariel muttered darkly watching as a truck peeled out from the airport. Carmen didn't bother turning on the lights on her bike. She pulled the fast but quiet Yamaha YAF-R1 motorcycle after it, popping up onto one wheel when she floored it.

"On it," Cara said shakily moving toward Abby's truck. Within seconds she had the engine running. When Ariel and Trisha jumped in the front seat and looked at her in a funny way, she couldn't help but add, "I used to have a problem with taking vehicles for a spin."

Cara slid the truck into gear and tore off after Carmen and the truck. "Call Carmen, ask her which direction."

Ariel pushed a button on her cell phone and within seconds Carmen answered. "He's headed north on the highway toward the mountains. I'm on his tail but he can't see me. I'm running dark."

Ariel couldn't help the shiver that went down her spine. "Carmen, don't play around. I need you," she added softly. She was afraid Carmen was going to do something stupid. She had been taking more and more risks lately, almost as if she were daring death to come get her.

"Just cover me. I'm not going to let anything happen to her," Carmen said.

"Should we call the local authorities?" Cara asked as she turned the wheel sharply, punching the gas pedal as far as it would go. "Damn, I need to work on her truck. The acceleration on this thing sucks."

Trisha rolled her eyes. "Only you would be thinking about something like that while chasing down bad guys in the middle of nowhere."

"Hey, I can work on more than one thing at a time," Cara said as she took another turn, sliding the truck around and fishtailing a little.

Both Ariel and Trisha let out a string of expletives they had learned while in the Air Force. Cara just laughed. She had taken more than one joy ride in her life and never been caught by the police who had been chasing her.

* * *

Zoran communicated with his brothers at a high pitch undetectable to human ears. *"Abby is hurt. I felt her pain before darkness descended."*

"Can you find her?" Kelan asked as he glided up beside Zoran.

"Yes. The symbiotics are trying to heal her. They are too small and too young to do much. They will try to help her as much as possible. They are sending a signal to mine which is directing me," Zoran replied, trying to keep the rage and fear out of his voice. He would kill the man who had hurt Abby.

"Do you know who it is?" Trelon asked as he flew up on the other side of Zoran.

"Yes. It is the same man who has been after Abby for years. He had become more aggressive over the past week. He wishes to claim Abby for his own. I will kill him," Zoran said with a growl.

The three dragons flew low down the side of the mountain, veering in and out through the tall trees toward the highway below. As they came over one last group of trees they saw headlights moving down the highway at a high speed. Swerving into a deep dive, Zoran collapsed his wings to give him speed before pulling up at the last minute as the truck suddenly hit its brakes and turned onto a side road. Zoran let out a curse as he swept up in an effort to slow his descent.

"There's someone following him on another transport, no lights," Kelan said behind Zoran, his huge wings pushing down air as he held himself still above the trees.

Zoran saw a figure on a small dark transport slide at the last minute to take the turn onto the road. *"If they mean to help him harm my mate, kill them,"* Zoran growled.

Pushing up over the trees, Zoran, Trelon, and Kelan followed the lights weaving in and out of the darkness. There was not enough room for them to land safely in their dragon form as yet. Zoran reached out again for Abby but all he felt was a frightening blankness where her warmth had been before.

"Trelon, fly ahead and block the road up ahead. Wait for us there. Kelan, fall behind. I heard another vehicle approaching at a high rate of speed. We will trap all of them together and kill them," Zoran said focused on the truck.

"What of you?" Trelon asked.

"I think it is time to introduce myself to those who mean to harm my true mate," Zoran said with a snarl before diving down through the trees.

Trelon flew just ahead of the truck and spewed a concentrated burst of dragon fire at the base of the trees along each side causing them to splinter and fall across the road. Kelan curved back along the road toward the vehicle coming up behind them. He did the same, trapping all the vehicles between the fallen trees. There was no place for anyone to go but through the woods. It didn't matter; they had already been sentenced to death as far as the brothers were concerned.

* * *

Clay glanced at Abby to make sure she was still unconscious. He waited too damn long for her to lose her now. He was furious that she thought he would give up. When he saw her for the first time four years ago, he knew she was going to be his. He followed her around, letting everyone know she belonged to him. He enjoyed the game of the hunt. She never suspected he had placed tracking devices on her vehicles or tapped into her phone. He had placed motion detectors at the base of her driveway and monitored her mail to make sure there was no one else. He toyed with her. If her granddad hadn't died unexpectedly, he would have been dead by now anyway. Clay had already made plans to take him out. He wanted Abby to depend on him and no one else. She had grown even more beautiful over the last four years as he waited for her to blossom as he knew she would.

His body wanted to do things to hers she probably had never dreamed of. Things he had done to some of the women overseas when he was in the military. They could never pin anything on him, just suspected he was involved in the disappearance of the women. He made sure no one ever found the pieces that were left after he got done with them. He could feel himself getting hard at the thought of tying Abby up and taking her. He wanted to hear her scream his name as he took her hard. He wanted her to know she belonged to him. He would kill this guy, Zoran, who thought he owned Abby. His fists tightened on the steering wheel at the thought of someone else taking the innocence that had been his for the taking. He had waited, nurturing Abby into womanhood so he could claim her. He didn't know where the man came from or how he was able to get past all the surveillance equipment he had set up, but he had signed his own death certificate by touching Abby. Abby would have to pay, too. She should never have let another man near her. Clay glanced down at the mark on Abby's neck. The first thing he would do was burn it off. She would learn as she screamed from the pain of having her flesh burned that she shouldn't have let another touch her.

* * *

Clay let out a curse, swerving back and forth, as he felt something heavy drop into the back of the truck. Zoran dropped out of the sky above the truck, shifting at the last possible moment. He landed with a thump in the back of it. He ignored everything but the man driving the truck.

Clay tried to glance back, but he couldn't take his eyes off the road long enough to see anything. He turned around again, when he heard what sounded like a growl. Glancing back at the road, he slammed on his brakes as his headlights highlighted the trees blocking the road.

Zoran smiled grimly as he held himself steady as the truck came to a shuddering stop. He heard a soft expletive right before he saw the two-wheeled transport behind him lay down on its side, sliding to a stop with the figure on the back of it rolling over and over finally coming to a stop along the side of the narrow road in an effort to not run into the back of the truck.

* * *

"Shit!" Clay said, hitting the steering wheel in frustration. *First, the damn females at the airport, now this.*

His gaze moved to Abby who let out a soft moan. It was still a couple of miles before they reached the end of the road and another five miles until they reached the cabin he had been working on for the past four years. It was just as well she was waking up, because she was going to have to do some walking. He reached over, jerking her up against him. Tilting her head back, he brushed his lips against hers.

"Wake up, baby doll, time to do some walking. I have some plans for you," Clay said, sliding his hand down over one of Abby's breasts and squeezing it hard.

Abby fought through the haze that clouded her mind. She felt lips pressing against hers then a hand grip her breast, squeezing it hard enough that she cried out in pain. Fighting to get away from the pain, Abby's eyes popped open when she couldn't move her hands.

"No!" Abby cried out, trying to push herself up and away from Clay. "Let me go."

Clay gripped Abby's hair painfully in his hand. "Never. I told you, Abby, you belong to me."

Clay pushed open the door of the truck, pulling Abby across the seat by her hair. Abby let out another cry of pain, as she was pulled out of the truck. Unable to prevent herself from falling, she hit the ground hard. Clay was just bending down to pick her up, when he was yanked back and thrown against the trees in front of the truck.

Abby cried out again as gentle hands picked her up off the ground. "Hush, *elila,* I have you."

Abby heard Zoran as if in a dream. "Zoran? Clay…be careful, he has a gun."

"Too late, bitch," Clay said from behind Zoran pointing his gun at Zoran's chest. "So, you are the bastard who thinks you can poach on my territory. I planned on killing your ass. Doing it in front of Abby just makes it sweeter."

Zoran stood up to his full height with a growl, pushing Abby behind him. He felt both his and his dragon's fury at the male's claim on Abby. Abby whimpered behind him, trying to stay upright.

"You are sentenced to death for touching my mate," Zoran growled, taking a step toward Clay.

Clay, recognizing Zoran was somehow threatening him, pulled the trigger firing point blank into Zoran's chest. "Think you can intimidate me, asshole? You're the one that is dead."

Abby screamed as she felt Zoran jerk back against her. Two loud roars filled the air just as a body flew out of the air, tackling Clay from the side. Abby cried out in anguish as Zoran collapsed to the ground in front of her. Abby kneeled in front of him ignoring the fight between the two figures.

"Oh baby, no," Abby cried. "Please, help him," she pleaded with the symbiot around her neck and wrists. "Please."

Abby watched as the symbiot on Zoran moved rapidly down to his chest disappearing under his skin. In moments, she watched as the symbiot quickly healed the wound, pushing the bullet out of Zoran's chest as it moved in and out. Zoran's eyes flew open, narrow slits as he let out an unearthly growl surging to his feet. Abby looked up from the ground where she was crying, watching as Zoran shifted into his full dragon form. She had never seen him change in person, only in the shared images of his home world. Within seconds, two other dragons appeared on each side of where Clay and a figure in solid black fought viciously.

Clay swung, hitting the figure in black a wicked blow to the head and then the chest, breathing heavily as the figure collapsed in a still heap on the ground. He turned with a bloody knife in his hand toward where Zoran, who now stood in full battle armor as a dragon. His eyes widened as he took a step back in horror. He turned to find himself surrounded by two other dragons glaring down at him.

Zoran moved toward Clay with a deadly snarl. Clay's mouth opened in a silent scream, as he was encased in dragon fire. Soon, nothing remained of him but black ash mixed into the muddy soil of the road.

All three dragons turned as the truck, which had been following Clay, came to a screeching halt. Zoran recognized Abby's truck. The doors flew open and three females rushed out, only to stop in shock as they saw three dragons. Cara was the first to respond.

"Holy shit! And I thought the little gold guys were cute," Cara said before glancing at the dark figure lying motionless on the ground. "Ariel... Carmen."

Ariel let out a cry, ignoring everything but the still figure on the ground. Kneeling next to Carmen, she turned her over, pulling the dark cap from her blonde hair. A large bruise graced the side of her left cheek, and a trickle of blood flowed from the corner of her nose and mouth. Trisha moved cautiously toward Ariel, while Cara moved toward Abby.

Ariel looked up at the three dragons. "Please, can you help her? Please..." she sobbed. Carmen had blood on her shoulder and chest where Clay had stabbed her. "Please...she's my sister. Help her."

Zoran looked at the still figure. He growled to Kelan and Trelon to take the injured woman and the other two women to the warship. He turned to growl at the tiny woman who had rushed to Abby's side.

"Back off, you overgrown lizard, or I'll have you for dinner," the little figure said as she quickly undid the handcuffs on Abby's wrists. When Abby looked at her silently, Cara shrugged, "I've had to get out of more than one pair in my life. Unfortunately, never in a good situation, can you figure that?"

Abby couldn't help the chuckle that escaped her. Only Cara would threaten a dragon while explaining how she could unlock a pair of handcuffs without a key. Cara helped Abby stand, holding her steady. She jumped when a male hand suddenly appeared.

"Shit! What the hell is going on?" Cara asked looking up at Zoran who stood towering over her. He gently picked Abby up in his arms as she swayed.

"Unfortunately, you have seen too much, little one. You will accompany us," Zoran said right before he and Abby disappeared.

CHAPTER 14

Zoran yelled out orders as soon as they materialized on the ship. Two men quickly came toward Cara while Zoran carried Abby down a few short steps and toward a door. Abby had lost consciousness again and was lying limply in Zoran's arms. He moved with lightening speed toward the medical unit.

"My lord, we have stabilized the other female. She should be all right. The other two females were taken to a holding room until you tell us what you wish to do with them," Jarak his chief of security explained as he followed Zoran to medical.

Zoran frowned but never broke his stride as the doors to medical slid open. "What of the other female who came with us."

"Trelon is working with her. She is not as…cooperative as the other two," Jarak responded hesitantly.

Zoran just nodded. Let his brother deal with her. He had enough to deal with worrying about Abby. He called for his mother symbiot. He gently laid Abby down on a medical bed. His mother symbiot burst through the door in the shaped of a huge mountain cat. It moved past him to where Abby was lying so still and pale. It purred as it brushed against Abby, splitting to form a smaller cat, which jumped up onto the bed next to Abby, laying down on her chest and stretching out. Zoran ran his hand down it.

"Take care of her, Goldie. She is everything to us," Zoran whispered softly, sinking down in a chair next to the bed. He would not move her again until he knew she was safe. Lifting her delicate hand, he wrapped it in both of his hands praying for the first time since he was a child to his gods and goddesses that his true mate would be all right.

* * *

Abby moaned as she relived the moment when Clay shot Zoran. She wanted to die. She had no reason to live without him. If a bullet didn't take him away then his brothers would. She knew she could never survive without him. Seeing him lying in front of her, a bullet to his chest had shown her that. She just wanted to sink into the dark oblivion and never wake up.

"*Elila*, wake for me. I miss you," Zoran said, brushing the hair back from Abby's forehead.

She had been unconscious for two days. His symbiot said she was just sleeping, afraid to wake. Her symbiot had grown as it absorbed more from its mother. Now, large gold bracelets adorned both of her wrists, as well as around her neck and ankles. Zoran could feel his dragon's impatience for Abby to wake as well. It clawed at him to get out, to call to its mate to see if she would respond. Unable to think of what else to do, Zoran let some of his dragon's breath wash over Abby before he gently bit her shoulder and breathed into her blood stream.

Warmth engulfed Abby's body right before she felt a sharp sting on her shoulder, followed by an intense burning pleasure. Try as she might to resist waking, the desire burning in her refused to let her remain unconscious any longer. She could feel something stirring deep inside her fighting to get out. With a loud cry as a hot wave of desire rushed through her, Abby's eyes opened as she panted until the wave crested and began to roll back out.

"Zoran," Abby cried out huskily.

"Shush, *elila*, I am here." Zoran smiled with satisfaction.

He could feel Abby's response. Even better, he could feel the dragon in Abby respond. She was still not ready to transform yet. Her body would need more time to learn how to. Zoran looked forward to teaching her.

Abby turned her head toward Zoran, confused. "Where am I?"

"You are in my cabin aboard one of our warships. We are on our way to Valdier," Zoran said softly kissing Abby's forehead as he continued to brush her hair to one side.

"But..." Abby looked around confused. "My mountain—"

"Will belong to someone else now, *elila*. You belong next to me, Abby. Now you will live among my mountains," Zoran said brushing a kiss along Abby's jaw.

Abby closed her eyes as another wave of desire began building. She began panting as it built even hotter. She opened her eyes, which had narrowed to elongated slits and stared at Zoran.

"What's happening?" Abby whimpered. "I feel the heat inside me building."

"You would not wake, and my dragon was impatient for you. He wants you," Zoran whispered against her lips. "So do I."

Abby moaned and blushed at the same time. "I need a shower."

Zoran laughed and pulled the covers off of Abby. She was naked. Abby gasped as she felt the cooler air of the cabin before Zoran picked her up and carried her into the bathroom. He gently set her down, watching her as she held onto the side of the cleansing unit.

"I will help you," Zoran said with a glitter in his eyes. Abby blushed as she saw the way Zoran was looking at her. She felt the wave of heat building even stronger as her body answered his call.

Abby stepped into the cleansing unit, turning to look at Zoran as he removed his clothes. She couldn't resist reaching out to touch his chest where Clay had shot him. The skin was smooth to her touch. Her eyes shimmered with tears as she looked up into Zoran's eyes.

"I didn't want to wake up. I was afraid you would be gone. All I could see was blood covering your chest," Abby whispered, moving into Zoran's embrace as he joined her in the cleansing unit. "I was afraid I'd never see you again and didn't want to have to face a life without you."

Zoran's arms tightened around Abby. "I am not easy to kill and could never leave you behind, Abby."

Abby groaned arching into Zoran as another wave of heat built so hot she felt like she was going to burst into flames. Abby couldn't contain the moan as she felt the damp heat between her thighs grow until moisture was beginning to run down the inside of her thigh. Her nipples were so sensitive, even touching Zoran's chest caused an intense pleasure/pain.

Abby pulled back enough to slide down Zoran, running her hands down along his side as she knelt in front of him until she was level with his cock. She watched as it grew even harder as her hot breath caressed it; beads of pre-cum glistened from its head. Abby leaned forward licking the tip of Zoran's swollen cock with the tip of her tongue, tasting his musky scent. Zoran groaned loudly as he watched Abby tease his cock.

"*Zi*, Abby," Zoran moaned pressing against her lips. "Take me deep, *elila*."

Abby opened her mouth, looking up at Zoran as he slowly pressed his cock between her lips. Zoran gasped at the sight of Abby taking his cock deep into her mouth. A wave of heat flashed through him as she cupped his balls in one hand while running her nails down the curve of his buttocks. Abby teased the tip of his cock over and over, pulling out to run her tongue along the slit before sliding the length back into her hot, moist mouth. Zoran ran his fingers through her hair, groaning as she played with him, taking him slowly. He felt his balls draw up tight as he shook with the need to explode into her. Gripping her hair, he pumped in and out of her mouth frantically, letting out a hoarse cry as he came. He watched as she drank, licking the drops from his cock while he shook from the touch of her tongue.

Zoran had to have her. He had been so frightened at the thought of losing her, he felt the need to claim her in the most primitive way. Reaching down, he drew Abby up against his body before turning her around to face the back of the cleansing unit. He drew both of her arms up and placed them against the wall so she was facing away from him.

"Ah, Abby, you are mine, *elila*. Tonight and always I take you as my true mate. My love for you will be burned into your soul as yours will be burned into mine," Zoran said as he stroked Abby's back and hips enjoying how she instinctively spread her legs wider for him to take her.

"Zoran," Abby whimpered feeling the burning wave cresting. She cried out, pushing back toward him.

Zoran used his mouth to tease Abby, nipping and tasting her as he possessively ran his hands over her. He wanted to touch her, memorize every nook, every dimple on her body. Abby pushed back against his fingers as he buried them inside of her hot sheath. He rubbed against her clit while his other hand moved to clasp her swollen nipple between his fingers. He felt the wave of dragon heat flow through her as she pushed against him. Not wanting her to come just yet, not until she gave him the promise he sought from her, he withdrew his fingers. Only then, would he let her find relief.

"Noooo!" Abby wailed, jerking as she felt Zoran bring her to the precipice before stopping.

"Say you will never leave me again, Abby," Zoran demanded softly against her neck.

"Take me Zoran," Abby moaned.

"Say you will never leave me again, Abby," Zoran repeated as he pushed two fingers deep into her. "Promise me."

"I promise," Abby cried out. "I won't ever leave you again. Please, Zoran, I need you."

Zoran smiled. "Not yet, but soon you will."

Abby glared over her shoulder at Zoran. "Fuck me now, dammit."

Zoran laughed softly as he slid into Abby's hot pussy, closing his eyes as he felt her wrap around him. He would never grow tired of the feel of her wrapped around him. Moving slowly at first, in and out of her, he wanted to savor the feeling of her hot sheath. He had plans to love her throughout the long night.

CHAPTER 15

Abby was still in a daze as she watched Zoran talk with his two brothers and his head of security. She was sitting on Zoran's lap. She blushed profusely when they walked into what appeared to be a conference room and found three huge men staring at her like she was a tasty morsel. It hadn't helped when she tried to move to sit away from everyone only to find herself firmly entrenched between Zoran's muscular thighs. She wiggled, trying to get free, until she felt Zoran move his hand between her thighs. When she tried to move his hand, he took his other one and slid it up under her shirt.

"What are you doing?" Abby whispered furiously, trying not to look at the three other men.

"If you insist on wiggling your ass on my cock, I will take you here right now," Zoran murmured in her ear.

"The others will see you." Abby glanced under her lashes at the men who were watching with interest.

"They wish to see how your species responds. They want to watch as I take you," Zoran said huskily.

Abby froze in horror. From the feel of Zoran's cock under her ass, he seemed turned on by the idea of others watching as he took her but Abby didn't feel the same. She began shaking as fear set in.

"Zoran, please don't," Abby begged. "Most of my species are very private about what we do. I'm very private. I don't think I could ever forgive you if you did."

Zoran frowned as he felt Abby begin to shake in his arms. He had not meant to frighten her. His species found nothing wrong with the enjoyment of watching others enjoying themselves. He would not offer to share Abby as she was his true mate and his dragon would not share. His brothers asked if they could learn how to please a human female as both expressed an interest in two of the females who were taken. He had not been offended. He found it rewarding to watch his brothers with other females, often suggesting ways to pleasure them. He would enjoy doing things to Abby they might suggest.

"It is not unusual for my species to enjoy watching others as they seek pleasure. It often heightens our own," Zoran said trying to calm Abby. If anything, her shaking became worse.

"Zoran, all is well with your mate?" Trelon asked curiously. "I smell fear on her."

Zoran pulled Abby tighter into his arms, frowning as she buried her face in his neck and clung to him. "Her species does not allow others to see them when they pleasure each other. Abby says it is a private matter between the mated pair."

"But..." Kelan began, frustrated.

Jarak leaned forward. "If the female is uncomfortable with my presence, I can leave."

Abby peeked out from Zoran's neck, tears glittered on her eyelashes. "It's not just you," Abby said softly. "Most people, humans, are very private about sharing their bodies. We don't walk around naked, we definitely don't make love in front of other people, and we don't share our bodies. Not all humans, but most find it offensive to even ask them to do so."

Abby looked up at Zoran sadly. "I'm afraid we didn't have much time to get to know each other; otherwise you would know this. If you don't mind, I'd like to go back to our cabin. I...I'm not feeling very well."

Zoran frowned down at Abby. He could feel her pain and it confused him. She was looking very pale. Perhaps, she reacted badly because she was still tired. Zoran felt a wave of disgust when he thought about how much she had been through a lot and how selfish he had been with his own desires.

Nodding, Zoran stood and picked Abby up in his arms. "I will return shortly. I wish Abby to rest more."

Abby didn't say anything as Zoran carried her back to their cabin. When he laid her down on the bed, she rolled over giving him her back and closed her eyes. She refused to cry in front of him. Zoran sat next to her for a moment, rubbing her back, before he leaned over giving her a kiss on her neck.

"I will return soon. Rest and we will eat when you awake," Zoran said, resting his hand on Abby's hip for a moment before he stood and left the room.

Abby listened as the door closed behind him; only then did she let the tears fall. What had she gotten herself into? Zoran's world and hers were so different. How was she ever going to fit in? It was more than just the sex in front of people. It was losing everything she had ever known and going into a world where she didn't know anything. What would happen if Zoran decided he no longer wanted her? What would happen if he wanted to have sex with other women? Abby knew she could never live with him if he did that. But where would that leave her? On an alien planet away from everyone she had ever known and loved and away from her beloved mountain. Abby cried until she was so exhausted she couldn't keep her eyes open. Slowly, sleep claimed her, giving her a measure of peace.

* * *

Zoran glanced across the table, worried, as Abby picked at her food again, pushing it from one side of the plate to the other, never eating more than a bite or two. She was losing weight and dark shadows appeared under her eyes. She seldom talked to Zoran unless he talked to her first. They had been traveling for over two weeks, and she became quieter the closer they got to Valdier. He reached out for the symbiot on her wrists to see if they would tell him anything, but as soon as he connected with them, they withdrew from him.

Slamming his hand down on the table, he watched as Abby jumped, "What is wrong? You must tell me, Abby. I watch each day as you fade further and further away from me."

Abby refused to look Zoran in the eye. "I've never turned you away." And she hadn't, she couldn't. Every time Zoran touched her, she felt the waves of heat build inside her, and she could no more turn away from him than stop breathing.

"You let me love you, but it is only to your body," Zoran said harshly. "You do not eat, you do not talk, you barely sleep. Why? You refuse to let me take you to medical, and even your symbiot will not answer my concerns. I need you to tell me what is wrong?"

Abby felt a tear drop onto her hand. "Nothing is wrong, Zoran. I'm just tired. That's all, just tired."

Zoran stood up, went around the table, knelt down, and gently lifted Abby's chin to look him in the eye. "You say that, Abby, but you do not sleep.

You think I do not know that you pretend to when I hold you at night. Tell me, *elila*, let me help you."

Abby stared into Zoran's eyes for a moment before she replied, "We are so different. We literally come from two different worlds." Abby laid her palm on Zoran's cheek. "I've lost everything I've ever known, everything I've ever loved; I've even lost who I am."

Fear made Zoran's eyes flashed with anger. "You are mine, Abby. I have claimed you. You will learn to adapt. You will learn to love my world, my people, and accept who you are now."

Abby shook her head tiredly. She had thought of nothing else but what she could do over the last two weeks, "Zoran, I don't belong here. I belong back on my mountain."

Zoran stood up, trembling at the thought of losing Abby. He had to get away. Walking toward the cabin door, he turned. "You are never going back, Abby. You will learn to accept what has happened. If you do not start eating, I will force you. If you do not sleep, I will medicate you so you get rest. You will learn that you are no longer the person you were."

Abby watched as Zoran stormed out of their cabin before replying, "Oh, Zoran, I'm not sure I'm strong enough to survive."

* * *

"I do not know what to do, Kelan," Zoran said as he nursed a stiff drink in his hand. "She is fading away right before my eyes. She doesn't eat, doesn't sleep, hardly talks to me. She wants me to take her back to her mountain."

Kelan swallowed his drink before pouring another glass. He was already well into his cups by the time Zoran found him. He picked up the glass and took another big gulp before replying.

"I am ready to take them all back!" Kelan slurred. "I have had it with her...them. They are bossy, opinionated, stubborn..." Kelan hiccupped, "and beautiful and too damn sexy."

Zoran frowned but before he could reply, Trelon came in growling under his breath. "I need a drink."

Before Zoran or Kelan could say a word, Trelon took the bottle of potent wine and started drinking straight from it, not even bothering with a glass. Wiping a hand across his mouth, he growled, "I'm going to kill me a tiny human female with red and purple hair. I'm going to rip her apart, burn her to ash, and then put her back together again so I can do it over and over until she begs for mercy."

Zoran looked at both his brothers. He had never seen them like this. "What is wrong?"

"Wrong? Wrong, he asks," Trelon growled, pointing the bottle at Zoran. "I'll tell you what is wrong. You landed on a damn planet of females who would drive any male to distraction and then act like it is the male's fault! No, you *couldn't* land on a planet where our symbiot would want to kill the female and our dragon would find them repulsive. No, you *had* to land on a planet where my symbiot is so infatuated with the female it does every damn thing she asks, regardless of what I say, and my dragon is so horny it is about ready to disembowel me if I don't claim her before another male does, only I can't catch her long enough to do so."

"You too?" Kelan looked burry eyed at Trelon. "My female refuses to even acknowledge me as a male. All she does is quote her name, rank, and some awful number I can't remember. She insists I take her home. My symbiot is sleeping with her like it is her new pet, sending me images of her stroking and scratching it and talking nonsense while me and my dragon get to suffer," Kelan grunted as his head fell forward. "She even said if I wanted to stay in my dragon form she would scratch my belly but she wouldn't touch me with a ten foot pole."

"What of the other females?" Zoran asked confused. What was happening to his brothers?

"The one named Ariel stays with her sister, Carmen. She is the female who was almost killed. She is a vicious one. One of the males from medical wanted her to mate with him. She knocked him out. They have been moved to their own cabin under guard," Trelon said taking another deep drink.

"Why are your females not under guard?" Zoran asked as he finished off his drink and reached for another bottle of wine.

"The one named Trisha is under guard, in my cabin," Kelan slurred. "Unfortunately, I can't get in because she has my symbiot attack me and drag me out every time I try to enter. Wait until I get her home. I am going to send my symbiot to play and as soon as it is gone, bam, she is mine!" Kelan giggled at the thought of finally having the female defenseless.

Trelon sighed heavily, "Cara has already hacked into the computer systems, engineering, communications, the environmental system, and our training programs. She had the men doing something called the 'Electric Slide' in the training simulator yesterday. The woman drives me nuts. I swear she never sleeps, never shuts up, and gets into everything!"

"Maybe Abby would feel better if she were to talk to some of the other females. Perhaps if she knew she was not alone, that others of her kind were here with her, she would feel better about staying," Zoran said perking up. "A dinner, I will set up a dinner for all the women. Notify Mandra to set it up. Invite as many males and mated couples as you can. Have Mother there as well. We arrive on Valdier tomorrow. Maybe if the females see that our world can be similar to theirs they will be more receptive."

"Oh joy, we get to be humiliated in front of everyone," Kelan said sourly.

* * *

Zoran felt better as he returned to his cabin. It would explain much if Abby was fearful of being the only one of her kind but she wasn't. There were four other females and she knew them. Perhaps if she knew that, it would help her. Opening the door of the cabin he moved in quietly, walking over to where Abby sat looking out into the blackness of space.

"It is beautiful, isn't it?" Zoran asked softly looking at Abby.

Abby smiled sadly. "I was raised to believe there was one god who created our world. Even that is something I can no longer hold onto."

Zoran turned Abby to face him. His heart was breaking at the look of bleakness in her eyes. "You can hold onto me, Abby. I love you very much, *elila*."

Abby looked into Zoran's eyes. "What does *elila* mean?"

"There is not an exact translation but it means 'my heart.' You are my heart, Abby," Zoran said softly brushing a light kiss across Abby's lips. "Feel my heart; it beats for you."

Abby looked at her hand lying against Zoran's chest right over his heart. A single tear coursed down her cheek. She loved him so much it hurt. She was torn between knowing she had to leave him and knowing she couldn't. She felt lost. She felt the warmth through his shirt, the soft thump of his heart.

"Now, feel yours," Zoran said taking her other hand and putting it on her chest. Abby looked up in wonder as she felt both their hearts beating at the same time. "How?"

"I told you, we are one now. I cannot live without you, Abby, just as you can no longer live without me," Zoran whispered against her hair.

Abby sniffed, trying to not cry. "Oh, Zoran, I love you very much. I just don't know. I don't know anything anymore."

"Know I love you, Abby," Zoran said, wrapping his arms around her tightly. "Tomorrow we will be on Valdier. You will see how beautiful it is. I have much to teach and show you."

Abby leaned into Zoran's warm body. She didn't want to worry anymore. She just wanted to feel his warm body wrapped around hers and feel safe in his arms. A soft sigh escaped her as her body finally gave in to all the stress and emotional duress she had been suffering over the last few weeks, and she fell asleep in Zoran's arms.

CHAPTER 16

Abby shivered nervously as she followed Zoran toward the transporter room. They had reached Valdier a couple of hours ago. Zoran had been busy with making final arrangements on board before he came to the cabin to get her. Abby was wearing the jeans and t-shirt she had on when she had been on Earth. She needed something familiar to help her deal with all the changes.

"So, how does this thing work? Are all my body parts going to be in the same place after you zap us? What does this button do? Why is that one flashing? Man, I'd love to take this puppy apart and see what makes it tick." Abby heard Cara's voice going a mile a minute.

Abby chuckled when she saw Cara moving like a hummingbird around and around the console holding the transporter controls, a symbiot following her while Trelon moved from one side to the other trying to catch her. Every time he would get close to her, Cara would either turn at the last minute just out of arm's reach or the symbiot would get between the two of them. Trisha stood over to the other side with a stony stare on her face, Kelan's symbiot lying at her feet with Kelan sending dark looks at her every now and then. Ariel and Carmen stood to the other side with two guards staring at both of them with lusty looks. Carmen bared her teeth at the guards, causing both of them to take a step back.

Abby touched Zoran's arm. "I didn't know you had brought the other women here," Abby whispered.

Zoran smiled down at Abby's surprised face. "I am afraid I have not taken as good of care of you as I should have. I've kept you to myself these past two weeks. It was necessary to bring them. They saw too much. Besides, the one named Carmen had been hurt too critically to leave her behind." He didn't add how he hoped having others of her with her would help her adjust.

"But..." Abby looked at the other women hesitantly. "Did they want to come? What if they want to return home?"

"This is their home, now, Abby. They cannot return," Zoran replied sternly. He did not want her to think if the others wanted to return to Earth then she could.

"But..." Abby started to argue, stopping at the dark look Zoran gave her.

"They will adjust just as you will," Zoran said before turning away to nod toward Kelan and Trelon to show he was ready to transport.

Taking Abby's arm, he guided her over to one of the transporter modules, holding her tightly as the lights began moving around them. In a matter of moments, they were on Valdier in the transporter room of the main base. Several guards appeared, bowing to Zoran as he pulled Abby through the room.

Abby glanced around the elaborate room she had been guided to before Zoran kissed her, promising to return later. He told her he ordered some clothing for her and a seamstress would be along shortly for her fitting.

Abby bit her tongue, trying not to give into the anger building inside her. She was getting tired of Zoran's high-handed attitude of bossing her around. She paced back and forth clenching and unclenching her fists. The more she paced, the madder she got. How dare he bring the other women here? Didn't he understand how it felt to lose everything you knew? Didn't he care if they had families who would worry about them and miss them?

She was the one responsible for Cara, Trisha, Ariel, and Carmen being here. It was her fault. If she hadn't invited them to her home, they would have been safe. Abby wrapped her arms around her waist. She had to talk to them, see if they were happy; if not, she had to find a way to talk Zoran into returning them to Earth. He had to listen to her. She was so tired of him telling her she would adjust. How would he know? He wasn't the one who had been ripped away from everything he knew. He wasn't the one having to rely on someone else for his very existence.

Abby was so upset, she didn't even notice the small scales that had appeared on her arms. Abby ran her hands up and down her arms as she felt the tingling grow under her skin. Moving toward the open double doors leading to the balcony, she looked out over the mountainous terrain towering over the city. Her eyes were drawn to a commotion down below her. A small figure was running across the expanse of purple grass far below, when suddenly a huge golden creature resembling an eagle swooped down and picked it up. Abby couldn't contain the gasp from escaping her as she covered her mouth with one hand trying to following the huge creature as it came higher and closer to her balcony. She jerked back as she saw the huge eagle was making a path straight for her. Abby's eyes got even bigger as she realized the small figure was, in fact, Cara who was yelling insults at the very aggravated male who was shaking his fist up at her.

Abby gave a small squeak as she jumped to the side as the huge eagle came even with the balcony, swinging back as it gently tossed Cara's small form onto the narrow area.

"Hi!" Cara grinned up at Abby.

"Hi!" Abby responded, startled to see Cara grinning with a mischievous Cheshire grin. "What on earth is going on?"

Cara looked over the edge of the balcony and with a laugh shot the still yelling figure below her a symbol using her middle finger. From the answering roar, the symbol was understood. "Just having a little fun," Cara replied cheerfully.

Abby leaned over the edge watching as the figure below fought with two other figures trying to hold him back. "Do you think it's wise to provoke him that way?"

Cara just grinned, never taking her eyes off the struggle down below. "It does him good. You know, he is the only man I have ever met that I haven't been able to drive away." Her gaze softened as she watched him break free.

Abby watched the emotions flowing across Cara's face, "You like him, don't you?"

Cara looked up startled. "Does it show? I love it here. I've only been here a few hours but I've never felt so free, so...right."

Abby watched as a thoughtful look passed through Cara's eyes. "How do you know you'll be happy here?" Abby asked softly.

Cara looked down as Trelon turned into a dragon. A huge grin spread across her face right before she let out a loud whistle. Climbing up onto the railing of the balcony, Cara glanced at Abby before jumping on the back of the huge golden eagle, "I don't know, but I'm willing to try. I've never felt this way before, and I'm not about to let it go without a fight...or two," she said before the huge creature broke away with a huge sweep of its wings. "I'll see you later at the dinner," Cara yelled before the bird flew into a dive barely missing the dragon coming up below it.

Abby shook her head, laughing, as the dragon let out a roar of outrage as it twisted at the last minute in an effort to avoid a collision with the massive bulk of the bird, a tiny, laughing human female clinging to its back.

* * *

The rest of the afternoon flew by. The seamstress came by with a legion of helpers carrying bolts of fabrics. She measured Abby, clucking her tongue as she muttered under her breath. It took Abby a while to convince the seamstress to create not only the dresses Zoran asked for but pants, shirts, and a variety of underclothes. Abby had to finally threaten to not wear a thing that was made if the order did not include panties and bras. Abby learned quickly that such items were not common attire on Valdier.

Abby was happy to hear the seamstress had also visited with the other women, excluding Cara, who was still on the loose, and clothing for them had already been ordered. Shortly after the seamstress left, a young man appeared at Abby's door.

"Yes," Abby asked, feeling sorry for the young warrior as he swallowed nervously.

"My Lady," the young warrior began, "Lord Zoran thought you might like the company of some of the other women who accompanied you to our world. He asked that I bring them to you, if that is per-per-missible," he finished with a stutter; a bright blush covered his face as he tried to keep his gaze from the dragon's mark on Abby's neck.

Abby smiled suddenly, feeling a very old twenty-two year old. "I would love the company. Please bring them by immediately. Oh, can you have some refreshments served as well?" Abby said as she watched him swallow and turn even redder.

"Yes, My Lady." The young warrior's voice squeaked as he saw the dimples appear in Abby's cheeks as she smiled. He turned, almost tripping over his own feet as he hurried down the passageway.

Abby just shook her head before closing the door. She was so confused. She had been so upset earlier, feeling guilty about being responsible for the other women being here and yet, Cara was so excited. *I don't know but I'm willing to try. I've never felt this way before, and I'm not about to let it go without a fight…or two.* Cara's words echoed through Abby as she recalled the look of hope and determination in Cara's eyes as she flew off. Lost in thought, Abby jerked when a sharp knock sounded on the huge wooden door dragging her back to the moment.

Laughter sounded as two out of the four of Abby's newfound friends and fellow Earthlings came into the room.

"Did you see the material and some of the outfits those women bought in?" Trisha was saying. Beside her was Kelan's symbiot, in the shape of a huge dog, following so close it brushed her leg.

"I know I'm going to look good tonight in that green creation. The men won't know what hit them!" Ariel was saying.

"Hey, Abby," Trisha and Ariel called out together. Both of them looked around curiously at the extravagantly decorated room.

"Wow, can you get over the size of this place?" Ariel asked as she moved aside to let by a young female servant who was carrying a tray of refreshments.

Abby moved over to the low table and made room for the tray, quietly thanking the young girl who quickly bowed and left, closing the door behind her.

"Hi. Come sit and have some refreshments," Abby said as she poured three cups of tea before she settled into a plush, cushioned chair near the window. "Isn't Carmen with you?"

Ariel let out a heavy sigh before shaking her head, "No. Carmen...is being Carmen."

Abby's long hair draped over her shoulder and down one side as she pulled her long legs up under her. "What does that mean?"

Trisha took another chair as Ariel sat down heavily on the couch across from Abby. "Carmen has issues," Trisha said.

Ariel gazed sadly out the window for a moment before she replied. "Not issues so much as just so much pain." Ariel took a sip of her tea before she continued. "She lost her husband three years ago and has never recovered from it."

"Do you think being here is making it harder on her?" Abby asked. She felt the guilt rise up inside her again.

Both Ariel and Trisha shook their heads. Ariel looked at Abby for a long moment before replying. "I think being here was the best thing that ever happened to Carmen. She can't run away here; at least not like she has been doing. She was looking for a way to die to be with Scott again. She can't do that here."

Trisha smiled mischievously. "I don't think Creon is going to let her get away with running anymore."

"Who's Creon?" Abby asked looking back and forth as Ariel frowned back at Trisha.

"Creon is a scary son-of-a-bitch…" Ariel began.

"Who has the hots for Carmen," Trisha finished stubbornly, "and is probably the only one who can break through the wall she has built."

Ariel glared at Trisha for a minute before letting out a sigh. "You're right, of course. Carmen would never have let go as long as she was back on Earth. I don't know if this Creon guy will be the one, but I have to agree he looked mighty interested when he first saw her."

"So…" Trisha asked looking at Abby, "do you know what this dinner tonight is about? And, has anyone seen Cara?"

Abby laughed as she explained what had happened earlier with Cara. It seemed as of fifteen minutes ago, Trelon was still trying to catch their nimble little dragonfly. "As for the dinner tonight, I don't know. Zoran has been very hush-hush about it."

The three women visited for the next hour before Trisha and Ariel made the excuse of having to go get "beautiful" for the evening. Abby thought back on the afternoon and had to admit she felt much better than she had in weeks. Sinking down into the fragrant water of the bathing pool, Abby realized her life back on Earth seemed more like a dream than a reality. She hadn't seen much of Zoran's world yet, but the little she had made her realize it was very beautiful and perhaps, just perhaps, she could be happy here.

CHAPTER 17

Zoran quietly let himself into his suite of rooms. His mother and Mandra had completed the preparations for the dinner. It had been interesting explaining how all the dishes being served to his mate needed to be free of any meat or meat products. Due to the nature of their dragon, meat was a mainstay for their bodies. He was not sure how Abby's dragon would handle her aversion to meat once the transformation was complete. The transformation…that was another issue he was going to have to explain to Abby. He was just worried about how she would handle it. Abby had been through many changes in just a few short weeks. He wanted her to accept his world and love it as much as he did. She was now its queen. How could he throw something else at her?

Walking through the bedroom into the bathing room, Zoran paused at the door drinking in the sight of Abby lying in the bathing pool. The crystal clear water swirled gently around her naked form. *Was it possible to be jealous of water?* Zoran thought as he felt himself harden. He was trying to give Abby some personal time. He was in meetings most of the day with his brothers and close security advisors going over the information Creon had discovered about his kidnapping. If the information was correct, then there were some serious threats to his people he needed to deal with immediately.

"Zoran, you're back," Abby said. She raised her arm up out of the water in an invitation for him to join her.

Zoran's eyes darkened with desire as he quickly shed his clothes. Descending the steps into the warm water, he pulled Abby into his arms, crushing her lips with his own. "You are so beautiful, *elila.*"

Abby gasped as Zoran grasped one of her nipples in his mouth and began sucking on it. "You aren't so bad yourself," Abby whispered. She quickly twisted around, pushing Zoran back against the steps and straddled his lap, slowly impaling herself on his thick cock.

Zoran let out a groan as he felt Abby's sweet warmth encase him. "Oh, *elila*, you are my life." Pushing up until his full length was buried inside Abby, Zoran wrapped one hand around Abby's neck pulling her down to capture her soft whimpers in his mouth while his other hand gripped her hip tightly in an effort to maintain what little control he had left. Abby couldn't stand the pressure, her blood burned with the need to ride him.

"Zoran, I...need...you," Abby groaned, feeling the heated waves of desire building stronger than ever. "Now...!" She screamed as a wave crested.

Zoran's eyes glittered brightly as he watched Abby's eyes change to narrow slits and her arms and chest began rippling with colors of pale blues, golds, and whites. A soft growl came from her throat as she threw her head back and began riding him faster and faster. He slid his hands up her back feeling her skin begin to change as the beginnings of her long wings began forming. Her dragon was making soft mating coughs calling to his as it fought to emerge for the first time. Zoran's own dragon was fighting to pull free as it tried to answer its mate's call. He gritted his teeth trying to pull it back. Now was not the time, Abby wasn't ready, even if her dragon thought she was. He needed to give her more time to adjust to living here first. Realizing if he didn't do something fast to stop her dragon from taking control, she would go through the change right there in the bathing pool; so he pulled even harder on his dragon. Zoran let out a dark growl of warning to Abby's dragon right before he sank his teeth into the junction between her shoulder and her neck in warning that he was the dominate mate and for Abby's dragon to submit to him.

Abby didn't know what was happening to her. She felt like she was on fire, her blood boiling. It was almost like there was something inside her fighting to get out. She could feel her skin tingling all over as wave after wave hit her. The skin on her back felt like it was ready to burst, as if thousands of little fingers were threading through scratching to get out. Small, strange sounds were coming from her, but she didn't seem to be able to do anything about it. It was like she was calling for *something*, begging for it to come get her, help her. She heard Zoran growl as if from a distance, and the sound sank deep into her, just as she felt the flash of pain and an explosion of desire so sharp she climaxed, a silent scream tearing from her throat as she convulsed around Zoran.

Zoran closed his eyes as he tasted the sweetness of Abby's blood flow into his mouth where he held her down in an age-old show of dominance.

He groaned as he felt Abby's climax wrapping a hard fist around his cock, squeezing him until he had no option but to release her neck and cry out as his own climax was forced from his body. He shuddered as he felt the hot jets of his seed release deep into Abby's womb. Zoran wrapped his arms around Abby's slender frame, pulling her down until she lay around his chest. He felt weak as a newborn babe as the last of his semen pulsed into her.

Zoran lay back with his head resting on the side of the bathing pool, his eyes closed as he gently stroked Abby's hair and back. He would never get enough of her. Neither would his dragon, which demanded that he let the transformation complete, since it wanted to be with its mate. *"Soon, my fierce warrior, soon you will be able to mate as I have done,"* Zoran reassured his dragon.

* * *

"I can't believe we're late," Abby muttered under her breath as she and Zoran hurried down the long corridor. "We would have been on time if you had kept your hands to yourself."

Zoran wore a silly, satisfied grin on his face. "But you needed help with your dress."

"Yes," Abby said, glaring up at Zoran, "getting it on, not off."

"But, *elila,* you look so beautiful without your clothes on..." Zoran said, his smile turning even more satisfied as he remembered how they ended up making love again even when they were trying to dress for the dinner.

He had done well keeping his hands off her after they finally got out of the bathing pool—until she turned around to have him tie the strips holding her gown on. The dark blue material accented her eyes, and when she turned her long expansion of creamy back to him he could not resist running his hands down it then under the soft material to cup her breasts. Now, due to that little distraction, they were running about a half hour behind when the dinner was supposed to start. He and his dragon had never been so satisfied. For that matter, Zoran thought with a huge grin, the beautiful gold symbiot didn't look too unhappy either, if the sparkles glittering from Abby's neck, wrists, and ears were any indication. Glancing down on Abby's dark, glossy curls piled high on her head, he could see the little sparkles of gold dancing back and forth across her skin, taking different shapes as she moved in quick little strides toward the open dining room.

"You need to behave yourself," Abby said sternly, stopping momentarily to put her hands on her hips for emphasis. "I will not be embarrassed in front of your mother, brothers, and god knows who else. Do you hear me?"

Zoran let out a laugh as he swooped down to brush a light kiss across Abby's lips. "I think everyone heard you, *elila*. But if it makes you feel better, I will try to control myself."

Abby raised one hand and gently placed it on Zoran's cheek while her other hand moved softly over the front of his pants. Rising up on her toes, she flicked her tongue along the seam of Zoran's lips. "Just until after the dinner," she growled softly before turning and walking into the large room.

Zoran felt his dragon growl in response to its mate's teasing. Adjusting the front of his pants, which had become decidedly tighter, Zoran groaned softly, "Our mate is not happy about us denying her. I have a feeling tonight's dinner will be a very long and painful one for the two of us." Zoran's dragon gave an answering growl of frustration as they both watched the soft sway of Abby's delectable bottom disappear through the door.

The sheer size of the dining room caught Abby by surprise, but its elegance took her breath away. Never had she seen so much glittering gold, striping the walls, accenting the tableware along the three long tables that had been set up in the center of the room, with staff in blue and gold uniforms, and all of the guests who were already seated dripping with golden necklaces, earrings, wrist bands. Even the light seemed golden as Abby took it all in, awestruck.

"Abby!" Cara squealed in delight.

Abby turned to watch as Cara approached her. Cara was dressed in a pair of dark trousers and a white top that hung low over one shoulder, baring it. Her dark auburn hair fell in waves around her small face, the purple highlights catching in the lights. What really caught Abby's attention was the length of chain, not the gold of a symbiot, but a long length of silver that wound around Cara's left wrist to Trelon's right one tying them together.

Abby gave Cara a quick hug. "Are you all right?" she whispered, looking worriedly into Cara's eyes.

Cara laughed, flipping Trelon a mischievous look. "Oh, there's nothing wrong. Lover boy here is under the impression that he has finally caught me and thinks a little ole chain will hold me to him." Cara leaned forward looking at Trelon while she whispered to Abby, "The fun has just begun." Cara smiled sweetly ignoring Trelon's growl of warning. Giving Abby a quick wave, Cara moved off pulling a furious warrior behind her as she danced in and out of the crowd introducing herself.

Abby jumped slightly when she felt a hand slide around her waist. "I think my brother has finally met his match," Zoran said in amusement.

"I certainly hope so," a husky voice said. "It appears that all of my sons may have."

Abby turned to see an older woman of incredible beauty watching in amusement as her oldest son turned a slight shade of red. "Mother, I am pleased you journeyed here."

* * *

Morian Reykill watched as her oldest son drew the small woman protectively to his side. She had arrived early hoping to observe each of the women who had been brought to their planet. Morian had to admit she was intrigued after hearing rumors that her oldest son had true-mated with a species different from any other known to their kind. She was impressed with the other women. Each one had her unique characteristics. Morian had fallen in love with little Cara, enjoyed the wit and intelligence of Trisha and Ariel, but she was concerned about the one called Carmen. She could sense a deep sadness in that one. But it was the one called Abby that she was most interested in meeting. It would take a strong woman to deal with her oldest. Now, she studied the delicate features of the girl who had obviously captured Zoran's heart. She let her gaze wander to the mark of the dragon on Abby's neck. So, it was true. A species not of their world had been accepted by a Valdier warrior, but even more remarkable by his dragon and his symbiot.

"Good evening, my dear. I am Lady Morian Reykill, high queen and mother to this motley group of misfits," Morian Reykill said with a sweet smile as she leaned over and gave Abby a kiss on both cheeks.

"Mother, you should not call me a misfit. I am High King, Leader of the Valdier, and a fierce warrior." Zoran frowned at his mother trying to imitate her fierce glare.

Morian let out a small chuckle "Yes, well...I remember too well what you and your brothers' bare bottoms looked like when I chased them.

Go get your mate and me some refreshments. I am simply parched from my journey."

Zoran let out a soft growl at his mother before brushing a soft kiss across Abby's forehead. "Don't believe a word she says. We were all perfectly behaved young boys."

Abby giggled as she watched Zoran hurry off to the long tables filled with all types of food and beverages. Listening to Zoran's mother pick on him and his brothers made her realize that maybe this world wasn't so different from Earth.

Morian looped her arm through Abby's, pulling Abby along after her as she moved toward a set of huge doors that opened onto a patio area.

"Zoran..." Abby said looking over her shoulder to where Zoran had disappeared.

"He will have no trouble finding you, my dear. I simply need to breathe some fresh air. It has been such a long time since I've been around so many others," Morian said moving farther into the softly lit garden area.

Abby looked around as she moved down the steps to follow Zoran's mother. The garden was breathtaking. Huge trees bordered one side, while steps continued down until they ended on the edge overlooking an ocean of green and white water. Flowers in every color imaginable, some the size of dinner plates and larger, seemed to glow, casting soft light around hidden sitting areas. Abby walked up to one of the flowers and gently touched one of the glowing petals. The flower closed up inside itself. Startled, Abby gave a squeak of surprise.

Morian chuckled as she watched Abby looking tentatively at another bloom. "I planted all of these many years ago. Most of the plants come from the area around my mountain home." Morian walked over to the bloom Abby had touched and gently spoke a few words in a low, musical voice. The bloom opened as Morian spoke to it.

"You have such a beautiful voice," Abby said softly, looking at the older woman with a mixture of curiosity and awe. "Do you sing?"

"Sing?" Morian asked. "Explain this to me?"

"It's when you say things but bring it together with a harmony. Sort of like what you just did," Abby explained.

"I do not know this *sing*. I use words blended with low sounds to speak to the plants. Can you give me an example of this *sing*? Do you do this a lot on your world?" Morian asked.

Abby blushed. She wasn't sure if the people here in this world would like her singing. She knew she had a nice voice. She had inherited it from her grandmother and grandfather. It wasn't even as if she was all that shy about singing in front of people, either, since she had sung in front of large groups in Shelby all her life. But suddenly, she didn't feel so sure.

"Sing for me, Abby," Zoran said as he moved down the steps toward his mother. He handed her a drink. "Sing for me the way you did on your mountain." He set down the drink he had brought for Abby on the ledge of the balcony and walked over to Abby. "Sing for me, *elila*.

Abby placed her hands in Zoran's, gazing into his eyes as she sang a short Gaelic love song she had learned a long time ago from her grandmother. When she finished, Zoran raised her hands to his mouth and gently kissed her knuckles. "Beautiful, *elila*. Just like you."

Abby blushed. She turned to look at Morian who was staring back at Abby with tears in her eyes. "I like this 'sing.' I would be honored for you to teach me."

Abby smiled at Morian, feeling another thread of her despair slowly dissolving as she realized a very important ally had accepted her—her new mother-in-law.

"Come, let us go eat and enjoy the festivities." Zoran smiled triumphantly as he realized Abby had moved one step closer to accepting his world. He wrapped his arms around the two most important women in his life and led them inside.

None of them saw the dark figures hiding high among the huge trees. One figure in particular remained focused on Abby until she disappeared from sight. Only then did the last dark figure move cautiously down the tree to disappear into the darkness.

CHAPTER 18

Abby gasped as Zoran gently set her down on the soft purple grass. It had been a week since the dinner where she and the other women from Earth were introduced to Valdier. Abby hadn't had much time to visit with the other women since then. She spotted them on occasion from a distance and had run into Carmen in one of the palace's long corridors while exploring. Carmen seemed nervous, as if she was trying to find a place to hide. She didn't say much to Abby other than that she was well and would talk to her later. Abby was puzzled about Carmen's behavior until she turned a corner a few corridors down and ran face first into Creon, Zoran's middle brother. Abby shivered as she remembered looking into Creon's cold, dark eyes. Abby had to agree with Ariel on the "scary son-of-a-bitch" description. He quickly excused himself and hurried off in the direction where Abby had last seen Carmen heading. She hoped Carmen would be all right.

"Oh, Zoran, this is so beautiful," Abby exclaimed as she moved toward the edge of a crystal-clear pool before gazing at the small waterfall feeding into it.

"I had hoped you would like it here," Zoran said as he came up behind Abby and wrapped his arms around her.

For the past week, Zoran had been debating about how to explain to Abby the transformation her body was seeking. Each time they made love, it was becoming harder and harder to keep her dragon from taking over. Hell, it was even harder for his own dragon not to demand it. It had only been his promise of explaining everything and then showing Abby how to complete the transformation by today that kept him at peace.

"Abby, there is something I need to tell you," Zoran began. He gently turned Abby around in his arms. He had picked this place because of its seclusion. He wanted Abby to feel comfortable in her first change. His mother symbiot was waiting for his command to appear. Once the change was done, he would divide his symbiot so her dragon would have the needed protection, but he hoped he could complete their first mating as dragons first.

Pulling back, Zoran raised Abby's hands to his mouth, pressing a gentle kiss to each of her fingers. "Abby—"

Zoran stiffened suddenly as pain radiated through his body.

"Zoran?" Abby felt Zoran's hands squeeze hers tightly and watched as his eyes darkened dangerously. "What...?"

Zoran thrust Abby behind him, ignoring her gasp of alarm when she saw the thick dart protruding from his left shoulder. Zoran let out a vicious growl, pulling the dart out before twirling around. He tried to shift into his dragon form but was unable to as a wave of dizziness flooded through his body. Grasping Abby by the hand, Zoran began running for the cover of the thick forest surrounding the small meadow, only to stop suddenly as dark figures emerged from the shadows. Zoran turned, but his path was blocked by more dark figures.

Abby was terrified. The huge, dark figures were close to seven feet tall. Black hair hung down to their waists. Their bodies were covered in a black leather with what appeared to be weapons strapped across their chests. Abby watched in horror as three of the figures raised a weapon and fired it at Zoran. She cried out as she felt Zoran jerk as three more darts hit him in his chest, shoulder, and leg.

"NO!" Abby screamed, holding on to Zoran as he slowly crumbled to the ground. "No, please, no!" Abby pulled the darts out of Zoran and threw them aside. "Zoran, oh baby, I love you." Abby ignored the approaching figures as she focused on trying to get Zoran to look at her. "Tell me what to do. Please, be all right."

A shadow covered Abby as she lay over Zoran's body trying to protect him. "So, we meet again, Valdier leader."

Abby looked up into the face of the dark figure. She shivered when she encountered cold, dead looking eyes. "What do you want?" she whispered.

"Something that should have been given to me several months ago," the dark figure said as he knelt down next to Abby and Zoran. "I do not like being denied what I want and now it seems you have two things I want: the secrets to your symbiot and a taste of your female. I wonder which will be sweeter." The figure laughed coldly as he removed a small syringe from a pocket of his jacket. "I will let you think on it while I sample at least one of the two."

Abby moved as if in slow motion, throwing herself at the dark figure before he could sink the syringe into Zoran. She felt the prick as the needle injected whatever was in the syringe into her side, even as she pushed the dark figure back and away. She heard a voice that sounded like hers but different as she attacked the figure with everything within her. Waves of despair and dizziness swamped her as she fought the hands trying to restrain her before everything went dark.

Zoran tried to roar out a challenge as he watched what was happening, but his voice and limbs refused to follow his directions. His dragon struggled to defend its mate but was unable to fight through the layers of paralyzed muscles that encased it.

The dark figure rose, wiping blood from his mouth as he smiled down cruelly on Abby's unconscious figure. "I will enjoy the taste of this one. She is a worthy mistress. Perhaps I will keep her for a while before turning her over to my men." His dark eyes turned to stare down at Zoran, laughing at the hatred staring back at him. "I was going to simply knock you out the easy way, but, unfortunately, that was the only syringe I had so I guess it will have to be the fun way. Just remember when you wake up what I want…the answer to how you control the symbiot. If I don't have the answer in three days time you will never see your female again—alive."

Zoran roared silently as he watched his hated enemy, the Curzian half-blood dark prince, pick up Abby's still figure and press a kiss to her mouth running his tongue back and forth across her lips. The last thing he heard before the blow to his head rendered him to the silence of darkness was Ben'qumain's cruel laughter.

* * *

"Zoran, come on, wake up." Creon patted Zoran's cheek a little harder.

"I don't think hitting him harder is going to wake him up, Creon," Mandra said as he watched Zoran's mother symbiot move to encase his brother's body.

"Whatever shit they gave him is powerful," Creon growled, turning to the third man standing back to the side.

The large figure was dressed in solid black leather. His thick, black hair hung down to his waist and was braided on each side to keep it out of his face.

"Trimida root. It makes one of the most powerful drugs we have to paralyze the wild gumbas on our planet. They are extremely dangerous, not to mention stink to high heaven, and meaner than my half-brother."

"Thanks for that non-needed bit of trivia, Ha'ven," Mandra growled sarcastically.

Ha'ven shrugged his shoulders, not in the least bit intimidated by Mandra's growl. "You're welcome. If his symbiot is as good as I suspect, he should be coming around soon."

* * *

Zoran heard the voices as if through a long tunnel, echoing at first, then becoming clearer and clearer, as he came closer to exiting it. He could feel his symbiot moving through his body purging the vile drug that held him captive. As more of the drug was forced through his pores, his head became clearer, and so did his memories. Zoran's symbiot burst from around his body, shaking as if to rid itself of the droplets of Trimida, just as Zoran let out a roar of rage shifting into his dragon shape.

"Oh, yeah. He's pissed," Ha'ven said warily keeping an eye on the furious dragon.

Zoran swung his head around, looking for the Curizan's voice. His narrow, slitted eyes focused on Ha'ven. A low, menacing growl rumbled in his chest as he slowly flipped over to a crouching position. He took a step toward the tall figure, waves of dragon fire building in his throat as he remembered Abby's still figure being carried away.

"Zoran, stop! He is on our side," Creon said stepping between Zoran's huge dragon and Ha'ven.

Zoran let out a deep growl, standing straight up to push his brother aside. Creon shifted quickly into his dragon. Snarling at Zoran, he warned him to stay back. Zoran ignored the warning, lunging forward and locking claws with Creon as he let a stream of dragon fire flow over Creon toward Ha'ven. Ha'ven rolled to one side raising a force shield in front of him, deflecting the dragon fire as it poured around him.

"*Enough!*" Creon yelled in dragon-speak. "*Enough, Zoran. Ha'ven is the one who has been helping us. I told you about our informant at the meeting. This is not going to get your mate back.*"

Zoran shook with the effort to get his dragon under control. The dragon was inconsolable at the loss of his mate. Zoran breathed deeply trying to calm his dragon enough to make him listen to what Creon was saying. *Calm, my friend. We need to listen to what he has to say if we are to rescue our mate. She is mine as well. I cannot live without her either. Calm.* Zoran kept repeating the message to his dragon until he finally brought it under control. With a shudder, Zoran shifted back, falling weakly to his knees.

"Zoran, are you all right?" Mandra asked calmly.

Zoran's eyes glowed as he stared coldly at Ha'ven. "Ben'qumain took Abby. He took my mate. I will kill the bastard. I will kill every last Curizan if he so much as harms a hair on her."

"Well, I guess that answers if he is all right. He is totally insane. Maybe you should lock his ass up until we get this mess under control," Ha'ven said with cool indifference.

"This mess, as you call it, asshole, is your brother's doing!" Zoran said rising to his feet, his fists clenched into tight balls.

"Not entirely," Creon said softly. "I think it best if we take this somewhere more private." Creon spoke quietly into a communicator and before anyone could say another word, all four men disappeared in a flash of light.

CHAPTER 19

Abby shivered as she slowly regained consciousness. She was disoriented, and her head felt funny, as if full of cotton. Shaking her head in an effort to clear it, Abby tried to sit up, but couldn't move her arms and legs. She pulled frantically and realized she was strapped down on some type of bedding on a hard surface. Abby looked wildly around as she tried to determine what had happened. She remembered Zoran being shot and collapsing.

"Zoran!" Abby cried out, tears filling her eyes at the thought of anything harming him.

"So, the Valdier's little pet has awakened," a voice said out of the darkness.

"Where am I? Where is Zoran? What have you done to him?" Abby forced the questions through a dry, scratchy throat. "Why are you doing this?"

Ben'qumain knelt down next to Zoran Reykill's delicious mate. Picking up a strand of her long dark hair, he pulled it toward him to sniff. "Beautiful. You are truly exquisite. I enjoyed the sounds you made the other night. Perhaps, I will keep you so you can 'sing' for me, along with other enjoyments, of course."

Abby shook harder, gritting her teeth; she stared defiantly into the cold eyes looking down at her. "When hell freezes over! Now, let me go!"

Ben'qumain laughed out loud. "You have much fire. I am going to enjoy tasting it."

Abby screamed as Ben'qumain grabbed the front of her shift and ripped it down the front. She fought against the restraints as he ran his hands down over her breasts to cup her between her legs. Recoiling against the touch of another man, Abby cried out frantically for Zoran as she twisted, trying to get away. Ben'qumain stood up slowly with a laugh and began pulling his clothes off.

* * *

"What the hell do you mean, Raffvin is behind this?" Zoran asked running his hands through his hair. All he could think about was Abby. "Raffvin was killed years ago, along with our father."

All four men sat around the conference table inside a Valdier freighter that had been modified into a small warship. The room was smaller than on the *V'ager* but still comfortable. In the center of the table was a holovid projecting a still image of Ben'qumain. Creon often used the disguised warship when he was working on assignments when he didn't want anyone to know what he was doing. The crew of the freighter consisted of hand-picked warriors Creon trusted with his life. Zoran was surprised at the mixed number of warriors consisting of both Valdier and Curizan.

"No, he made it appear he had been killed. In truth, he killed father and staged his own death. He had always been jealous of father," Creon said softly. "I had doubts when we could not find his body."

"It was during the same time my own father was killed in an 'accident,'" Ha'ven joined in, "that seemed very unlikely shortly after Ben'qumain appeared, claiming to be a product of my father and a servant's mating. My father was supposedly killed while on a hunt. There was little left of his body by the time we found it. I became very suspicious as Ben'qumain had been a member of the hunting party and was the only one to have seen the supposed attack of a pack of gumbas. My father was too experienced a hunter to have fallen prey so easily. After two more serious injuries involving two of my younger brothers, my brothers and I became extremely leery of the sudden 'accidents' that seemed to be plaguing our family. What my brothers and I have learned since is that Ben'qumain has gathered a small following of rebels in the hopes of killing us and taking over the ruling house of Curizan. He has joined forces with your Uncle Raffvin, who wants control of your kingdom."

"How do you know all this? How do you know Raffvin is involved?" Zoran asked coolly. He still could not believe that his uncle who had been like a second father to him as a boy would do such a thing.

Creon nodded to Ha'ven who turned on a holovid. "This was taken by an informant who is working for us. We both have men who have put their lives at stake to gain the information we have," Ha'ven said.

The holovid showed Ben'qumain talking to a group of men at what looked to be a military camp of some sort. The view was very narrow as whoever was taking it seemed to be at attention. Out of the corner of the holovid came another figure; as he came closer, his image became clearer. It was their Uncle Raffvin shaking hands with Ben'qumain.

"Greetings. You have set in motion your part of the plan?" Ben'qumain asked.

"Yes, but there is a problem. Zoran has survived. He is returning as we speak," Raffvin said sharply. "You were supposed to kill him!"

Ben'qumain gave an ugly laugh. "Yes, and you were supposed to give me the information I requested."

"I told you, only the ruler of the Valdier has access to the information you seek. It is written in the Chronicles of Valdier. Only the ruling king's symbiot has the ability to access the information. You were supposed to get the information on his symbiot so you could use it. No other symbiot has access to it!"

"He was being stubborn. He would not reveal where his symbiot was hidden and refused to call it to him, no matter how much we tortured him. There has to be another way," Ben'qumain growled impatiently. "It will do me no good if he is dead!"

Raffvin's face curved into a cruel smile. "My informants have given me information that may be useful. Zoran has found his true mate. There is one of two ways to get the information you seek. Capture his mate, and he will be forced to give it to you, or if it is true and the female is his true mate, wait until he gives her the protection of his symbiot. It will not leave her unprotected once he has given it to her. The problem with that is she will be stronger and it will be more difficult to control her with the symbiot's protection. It would be better to take her beforehand."

Ben'qumain looked thoughtfully for a moment before replying. "A true mate, you say?"

"A very lovely one from what my informant tells me. She could bring you much pleasure as well for all your troubles." Raffvin chuckled as he and Ben'qumain moved to far away for the holovid to capture any more.

Zoran swore softly under his breath as he stared at the still images in the holovid. He felt sick at the thought of what Abby must be going through. He had had a taste of Ben'qumain's torture. So help him, if Ben'qumain touched Abby, he would tear him apart limb by limb.

CHAPTER 20

Abby screamed again as she fought against the bonds holding her. Her skin tingled and itched as she struggled to break the straps around her wrists and ankles. She would not let him touch her! She would rather die than let another male take her. Abby felt a sudden wave of dizzying heat rush through her. She barely noticed Ben'qumain's sudden stillness as his eyes widened in surprise in the process of unzipping his pants. Her breath came out in pants and she noticed the dark room started to look clearer. She could make out the high, rough cut ceiling of a cave and the beginning formations of stalactites. Suddenly the straps holding her ankles snapped and she was able to twist over onto her stomach. As she pulled on the straps holding her wrists, she watched as pale blue, gold, and white scales appeared on her arms. Her hands began to curl and she watched with a mixture of horror and awe as claws began forming where her fingers had been. Abby closed her eyes and welcomed the next wave of fire that raced through her, inviting the wave as she felt her body shift and change.

Smooth scales formed over her body. Abby arched her back as she felt the tingling spread. She could feel a tearing sensation as her wings formed, pushing out in long, leathery perfection with small claws forming at the joints. Abby swung her head towards Ben'qumain and let out a low growl as the straps holding her wrists snapped like a rubber band stretched too far.

Ben'qumain let out a yell as he stumbled backwards falling over a rock and landing on his back. He scrambled backwards unprepared to face an enraged Valdier dragon. "What? This is impossible!" He breathed out. "You are not a true Valdier!"

Abby's face had changed as well. Her brow had broadened to accept the changes to her eyes which were protected by long, black lashes. Her nose lengthened and her mouth contained rows of small sharp teeth. Her throat burned. She narrowed her gaze on Ben'qumain's prone figure, images of Zoran laying defenseless on the ground floated through her mind and with a loud roar she opened her mouth and let out a stream of dragon fire before swinging around and moving swiftly towards the opening of the cave.

Ben'qumain let out a scream as he rolled trying to get away from the dragon fire. A long strip of his skin along his back smoked and blistered as the fire passed over him before he could get completely covered.

He screamed as his skin burned. "Kill her! Kill her!"

Abby moved awkwardly towards the entrance, letting out another stream of dragon's fire to push back the wave of men racing to the entrance. As they fell back, Abby could feel the muscles in her back legs tighten as if she were going to jump. With a downward push of her wings, Abby pushed off the entrance lifting as she went. She felt a sting in her left leg and another near her shoulder as the men on the ground opened fire. Letting go, she let the dragon inside her take over hoping it would know what to do. Abby retreated deep inside wanting to escape into a place she could understand and where she felt safe. Without Zoran, she no longer cared what happened.

Creon motioned to Mandra, Ha'ven, and Zoran to move forward with their men. They received the location of Ben'qumain from Creon's informant. The last transmission had been two hours before. They spent the last two hours fighting the thick undergrowth of the forest leading to the beginnings of the Hidden Mountains west of the Valdier City. The transports were able to drop them off along the river almost ten miles south of the site. Because of the thick growth, they were not been able to shift to their dragon form and because of the view from the caves, they could not fly in directly without being seen. In addition, they couldn't risk using the energy transfer from the warship for fear Ben'qumain would read the energy signals. That left them no other options; they had to cut across and through the forest in order not to be seen. If Ben'qumain hadn't taken Abby, they would have just blasted the hell out of the site. Zoran cursed silently as he and his group of five men moved forward through a particularly thick section. He could not stand the thought of what Abby must be going through. So help him, if Ben'qumain had hurt her, touched her, in any way, Zoran would shred him to little pieces.

Why did this have to happen now? He finally felt like Abby was beginning to accept being here on Valdier. That she finally accepted being here with him. He had been so worried about her while on the warship but in the last few weeks she seemed to enjoy being here. He wanted to show her how beautiful it was; show her how beautiful she was and finally, finally show her what she had become! Moisture burned the back of his eyes as he thought of how helpless he felt when Ben'qumain pulled Abby away from him and pressed his lips to hers.

"Zoran!" a fierce whisper called again.

Zoran jerked his head around to glare at Mandra. He had to get his mind back on what was happening here and now or he would be of no good to Abby. Mandra looked calmly at Zoran for a moment before nodding. With a jerk of his hand, Creon signaled he and his men were making the move up the west side of the mountain and for Zoran to take the east. Ha'ven and Mandra would follow up as soon as Abby was secured. Zoran gave a brief nod and motioned for the men to follow him. With deadly stealth, they moved up the mountain as the sun began to set on the second day of captivity for Abby.

The climb took almost an hour. Zoran had no trouble seeing as the skies began to darken. He shifted his vision so he could find the hand and foot holds he needed to pull himself up and over the narrow ledge that ran up to the caves. Pushing back as far as he could to blend into the side of the mountain, he didn't wait for the other men before he pushed ahead towards the faint glow of lights. He moved swiftly and silently up behind one man and with a quick jerk, broke the man's neck. Pulling him over to the side, he pushed the body into the shadows even further. He moved towards the front of the cave. Ben'qumain must have felt more confident than he should. There had only been two guards out front. He took care of one and Creon took care of the other. Zoran glanced over at his brother and nodded. Each man shifted into their dragon form, their symbiot forming armor around them as they crouched. Zoran glanced around the cave noting the position of each man, ten in all, sitting or laying around small artificial fires. Zoran's eyes narrowed onto one figure in peculiar, Ben'qumain, who was sitting without a shirt on near the back of the cave. Zoran's eyes narrowed with hatred as he watched another man use a med scanner on Ben'qumain's back. Ben'qumain jerked, cursing violently at the man before rising slowly to stand. Zoran could see a long line of pink, scarred skin running a path from Ben'qumain's right shoulder across his back and down to his hip. The skin looked new and traces of blood could still be seen. Zoran's lips curled back. Ben'qumain would have more than that before the night was over. Zoran frowned when he couldn't find any sign of Abby. He swung his gaze around and before he could stop himself, a deep growl erupted from his throat as he saw Ben'qumain stiffly bend down and pick up what remained of Abby's shift and throw it into one of the fires.

Ben'qumain's head jerked up when he heard the low growl. With a yell, he reached for a blaster on his hip. Zoran charged forward, confident his brother would not be far behind him. With a loud roar, Zoran and Creon each let out a stream of dragon fire at the men closest to them. The men didn't have time to pull up their shields before they turned to ash. In a matter of minutes, the fight was over. Ha'ven and Mandra followed quickly with the ten men Zoran and Creon had and they quickly over powered the small group Ben'qumain had. Ben'qumain took a blast to the leg and Zoran scorched him across his chest and arm. Zoran shifted all but one hand as he approached him. Wrapping a claw around Ben'qumain's neck, Zoran growled deeply squeezing the neck he held until the tips of his claw punctured the skin.

"Where is she?" Zoran growled menacingly.

"Dead!" Ben'qumain said with a nasty smile. "But not before I tasted her. Do you want to hear how she screamed as I took her?"

Zoran felt his dragon's roar of pain and outrage. Unable to control the unimaginable grief wielding up inside him, he dropped Ben'qumain and shifted letting the pain pour out of him in the form of dragon fire. He ignored Ben'qumain's screams as he burned him to ash.

Zoran shifted back before he turned numbly and walked to the entrance to the cave. He stared out into the night sky blindly. He didn't understand how he could even still be standing. It was as if his body didn't even exist anymore. Was it possible for the body to be alive while the rest of him was dead? He didn't even jump with he felt the hand on his shoulder.

"Zoran?" Ha'ven said quietly. "She is alive."

Zoran turned and stared blankly at Ha'ven. "What?"

"My informant says the female is alive." Ha'ven repeated softly.

"Where is he?" Zoran said, his eyes beginning to glow.

Ha'ven motioned for a young Curizan man of about twenty to come forward. "This is Kehid. He has risked much to help us. He was here when the female escaped."

Zoran looked at the young man who returned his stare calmly. "You saw her escape?"

"Yes, My Lord. She was in the shape of a dragon though. Ben'qumain had taken her to the back of the cave to…" Kehid cleared his throat. "There was nothing I could do to save her from that, My Lord. Ben'qumain had ordered us to stand outside. I am sorry."

Zoran closed his eyes fighting back moisture. Clenching his jaw, he opened his eyes and nodded for Kehid to continue. "Go on." Zoran choked out.

"Not long after, we heard screams. Ben'qumain yelled orders for us to kill the female. When we arrived at the entrance to the cave, a small pale blue, gold, and white dragon appeared breathing dragon fire. She flew off to the north, over the mountain." Kehid finished.

Zoran took a deep breath. Abby was alive and had transformed. All that mattered was she was alive. Zoran felt the change as his dragon roared for the right to find his mate. He would let his dragon take over. He would be able to sense where his mate was and would not stop until he had her safely under his wings.

"One more thing, My Lord." Kehid called out. "She was wounded. I do not know how badly."

Zoran's growl turned to a roar as he lifted off, flying straight up until he could turn to the north. His dragon scented the air, catching the faint odor of his mate's blood. Zoran spoke softly to his dragon. *Soon, my friend, soon she will be with us and we will never let her out of our sight again.*

Abby didn't know where she was. She flew as far as she could before the combination of blood loss and fatigue forced her to land in the first available opening. She had finally become a little more conscious of what was going on to her. At the cave, Abby as a person, had withdrawn so much inside herself that the dragon part of her took over. But, the further she flew, the more curious she became as to what was happening to her. At first, she was terrified! When she realized she was flying, Abby screamed, scaring the dragon part of her, causing her to tumble over and over before righting herself. Her dragon giggled at Abby's reaction. The further they flew, the more Abby began to realize her dragon was much like a young child looking out over a new world for the first time. Abby finally began to enjoy the feel of the cool, night air on her face and wings and the glitter of stars in the night sky. She could see at night as good as she could during the day. Eventually, the burning from her wounds began to seep into her consciousness and weariness pulled at her until she finally began the slow descent. She landed in a mountain valley that contained a long, narrow meadow. Abby limped, whimpering at the burning pain in her back leg and front shoulder. Lifting her head, she sniffed the air for danger. All she smelled on the gentle breeze was the aroma of wild flowers. Tilting her head, she heard the soft sound of water gurgling nearby. Abby limped over to the small brook and buried her nose in the icy water. Taking a deep drink, she slowly lowered herself down along the bank and began licking the wounds on her shoulder and back leg. The bleeding had stopped but both of them still stung. Laying back on her side, Abby gazed up at the stars and let out a series of small, coughing sounds. She knew her dragon was calling for help from her mate. Abby didn't have the heart to let her dragon know that her mate would not be coming. All she could do was whisper over and over to her dragon that everything would be okay, even as her own heart broke into little pieces. Her dragon knew of course. They were one and the same and her dragon could see the image of Zoran in the meadow, helpless. Large, silvery tears glittered, then slowly coursed down the cheeks of pale blue, gold, and white to fall like diamonds into the soft purple grass as Abby's dragon continued to call for her mate on the wind.

Zoran flew into the moonless night, slowing occasionally to swerve back and forth when his dragon lost the scent trail of his mate. It was strange, but for the first time, he felt the total connection of his dragon, symbiot and self as all three struggled not to be overwhelmed. He had covered almost two hundred miles from the cave when his dragon suddenly jerked as if shot. Zoran could feel his heart thundering as the soft sounds of a dragon's call reached him. Joy burst through him as he recognized the calls of Abby's dragon. It was the same soft coughing noises she made when her dragon was trying to emerge while they were making love over the past week. Zoran swept his eyes back and forth as he flew between two peaks and began a downward descent into a long, narrow valley. As he flew lower, the sounds of a dragon's soft cry of mourning reached him. There was so much pain and sorrow in the cry Zoran's dragon had to respond. He let out a long rumble of joy, calling to the female. Answering her with a mixture of low growls and deep rumbling to convey his need to love and protect her. As Zoran's eyes lighted on the still figure of the small dragon laying in the soft purple grass, he felt his heart swell with love at how beautiful she was. With a strong downward swept of his wings, Zoran landed a few feet from where Abby laid. Zoran moved quickly toward her, lowering his head to gently touch his snout to hers. When Abby's dragon tiredly raised her head to rub against him,

Zoran could no longer hold back tears of relief. Gently, tenderly, he moved his body closer to Abby's and spread his wings to enfold her against him as close as he could. Wrapped in his wings, he lowered his head and laid it across her neck, protecting her as she finally drifted off to an exhausted sleep.

CHAPTER 21

Abby dreamed that she was a dragon flying through the air. She moved in her sleep, snuggling closer to the warmth that seemed to surround her. Stretching out her legs, she smiled. She felt good and something smelled really, really nice. Moving her head without opening her eyes, she followed her nose, sniffing. *Mmm, Zoran.* He always smelled good to her. Brushing her mouth against his neck, she let her tongue move over his scales to taste him. *Mmmm!*

Abby's eyes flew open when she realized she was licking scales with a very long, narrow tongue. Lifting her head, Abby stared into a large male dragon's golden eyes. Zoran! She was wrapped in Zoran's wings, and he was in his dragon form! Abby blinked again and looked down at her body snuggled up against him. She was a…

"I'm a dragon!" Abby whispered in awe.

"A very beautiful dragon, elila," Zoran replied softly, brushing his snout against Abby's neck and licking her.

"But, how?" Abby turned to look into Zoran's eyes. *"How can I understand you?"*

"Dragon-speak. It is how we communicate with each other in this form. You are my true mate, Abby. You survived the dragon fire. You were accepted by my dragon and are the true mate to him. This is what I wanted to show you. Your dragon has wanted to transform for the past week. It was hard to convince her to wait." Zoran's eyes grew sad. *"The first transformation is the scariest, even for the Valdier. I wanted to be with you, to help you. I am sorry, elila."*

Abby leaned up and licked Zoran's mouth. *"I love you so much. When I thought you were dead…"* Abby couldn't continue.

She pushed herself up, wobbling a little as she adjusted to the feel of her new body. She glanced down at her shoulder and back leg. Both were healed. Abby noticed that she had what looked like a large low-hanging necklace of gold. Abby moved over to the small brook and took a drink before lifting her head high and shaking her body all the way from her snout to the tip of her tail. Looking over her shoulder, she spread her wings out wide behind her.

"This is so cool!" Abby said, laughing as she twirled around in a circle trying to see every part of her body.

Zoran's dragon let out a deep growl as he watched his mate raise her tail and flick it back and forth in an unconscious invitation. Zoran felt the wave of desire hit him quick and hard. He shuddered at the overwhelming feelings of desire and need to possess that came over him.

"Abby," Zoran growled again as he watched Abby's dragon duck her head down and stretch her neck in an invitation to dominate her.

Zoran moved closer, preparing to bite down and take Abby when, suddenly, Abby's dragon let out a snap and growl and leaped into the air away from him. Zoran's dragon let out a roar at the challenge. He felt the surge of primal need to capture and claim his mate and, with a powerful leap, followed the smaller dragon as she flew straight up.

"Abby! Submit to me. I claim both you and your dragon," Zoran roared.

"You have to catch me first!" Abby laughed as she swirled in the air, heading for the trees at the end of the meadow.

Zoran's heart swelled as he followed his little dragon. He chased her, giving her the lead as she flew in and out of the large branches, sometimes closer to them than he or his dragon liked. Whenever he got close enough to nip her tail, she would tuck it up under her little body and swerve. After almost half an hour of playing chase and tag, Zoran and his dragon had had enough. He wanted Abby with a hunger unlike anything he had ever felt before. Determined to bring her back to the meadow, Zoran cut Abby off, pulling his larger body closer to hers and forcing her to move out of the protection of the trees into the sky above, where he could safely pin her to him. He watched as Abby pushed through the top canopy of the trees into the clear sky. As he broke through, he put on a burst of speed, rolling, so that he came up under Abby's soft belly. Grasping her with his front claws, he pulled her, forcing her tightly against him. Zoran's dragon let out a low growl of warning as he bit down on her neck, forcing her to submit to him at the same time that he thrust up, impaling Abby to him. The only thing keeping the little dragon from trying to break free of his hold was Zoran's grip on her neck.

Abby was startled when Zoran's dragon grabbed her front claws twisting her around and locking her to him. She wanted to fly some more. She had never felt so free and wild. As she struggled to pull free, she felt Zoran's sharp teeth bite down on her neck, forcing her to stop. All she could do was flap her wings in an effort to break free, until she felt the long, full length of Zoran's dragon penis against her, fully aroused, before he flicked her tail to one side and took her. Abby felt the shock and desire as her dragon responded to her mate's aggressive possession. Each flap of her wings seemed to impale his hard penis deeper into her and a hot wave of answering passion flared. Zoran pushed down on Abby's neck, forcing her to slowly let him take control of her as he forced her back down to the meadow where they separated right before they landed.

"Mine!" Zoran and his dragon growled as he charged Abby's smaller form.

Abby's dragon spun around and swished her tail at Zoran almost hitting him, as she growled back. Abby giggled as she worked with her dragon to make it harder for Zoran and his dragon to subdue her. Every time he advanced, she hissed, spun, or thrust out with her tail, trying to keep him at bay. In turn, Zoran circled around, coming closer and closer, when Abby thrust out with her tail and Zoran grabbed it, flipping Abby onto her back. As soon as she was down, he pounced on her and held her down with his powerful claws, biting Abby's neck while his powerful tail twisted with her own, holding it out and away giving him easy access to her soft heat. With a deep rumbling groan, Zoran took Abby as his mate, locking himself inside her until they both collapsed, exhausted.

* * *

Abby awoke to find herself encircled in a pair of strong tan arms. She was human once more, she thought, with a tinge of regret. Her body felt so relaxed she wondered if she would ever be able to move again.

"So, my feisty little dragon has awakened," Zoran said, a hint of a smile lifting the corners of his mouth.

"Mmm, I feel so good," Abby murmured, snuggling closer to Zoran.

She couldn't resist running her hands up and down his chest. Soon, she was following her hands with her mouth. She loved the way Zoran responded to her touch. As she moved her hand moved farther down his stomach, a chuckle escaped at his gasp.

Abby lifted her head and smiled. "I'm hungry."

Zoran's eyes glowed as he wrapped his hands into Abby's hair. With a thrust of his hips, he groaned, "Then, please, eat all you want."

Abby chuckled again as Zoran slipped his hard cock between her lips. Pulling on the hard flesh, Abby couldn't suppress a groan of pleasure as the salty-sweetness of pre-cum touched her lips. She loved his taste. She loved everything about him. How protective he was of her. How much he tried to make sure she was happy. But, most of all, how much he loved her. She could feel the love he had for her and her dragon. Never would she have dreamed her life would change so much, that she would one day find and fall in love with an alien or that he would abduct her and take her so far away from her mountain. She had much to learn. She was no longer just Abby Tanner. She was Abby Tanner, a dragon, and true mate to Zoran Reykill, Leader of the Valdier.

"What are you thinking about?" Zoran groaned out as he gritted his teeth against the pleasure washing through him.

"How much I love being with you," Abby said softly as Zoran pulled her up so she was straddling him.

With a quick thrust, Zoran pushed deep into her, enjoying watching as her eyes half-closed and her head fell back as she took him into her body. Holding her hips, he thrust faster and faster reveling in the feel of her body gripping him tighter and tighter the closer she came to climaxing.

"You are mine, Abby!" Zoran growled out as he felt her fall over the edge taking him with her.

"I love you, Abby. I..." Zoran wrapped his arms tighter around Abby's slender frame, preventing her from withdrawing from his body. He took a deep breath before continuing. "I was afraid I had lost you. When Ben'qumain told me what he had done to you, I..." Zoran's eyes burned, and he couldn't finish what he was trying to say. A deep pain lanced through him, and he locked his arms even tighter around her as he pressed his face into Abby's neck.

"Sh...Ben'qumain didn't hurt me," Abby said softly as she pressed small kisses on top of Zoran's head. "He scared me. I thought he had killed you. That hurt me more than anything else."

Zoran shuddered and gripped Abby's face between his large hands. He looked up at her. "Abby, I know what he did. One of the warriors, Ha'ven's informant, told me about Ben'qumain raping you. They heard your screams. It doesn't matter. You are mine and will always be mine."

"Zoran, he didn't rape me." Abby tried to move.

"Abby, all will be well. I..." Zoran begged. He knew Abby was trying to protect him. He needed her to understand he knew she had no choice. He would do anything—everything in his power to help her overcome what happened to her.

Abby placed her fingers over Zoran's lips and looked into his eyes. "He didn't rape me, Zoran. My dragon wouldn't let him. She transformed before he could touch me. She burned him."

A shuddering sob escaped Zoran as he crushed Abby's lips to his own. He didn't know if he would have ever been able to forgive himself for not protecting Abby from Ben'qumain's evilness. Pressing desperate kisses all over Abby's face, Zoran rolled Abby over onto her back and made love to her frantically, desperately. She was alive, safe, and his.

CHAPTER 22

They did not return to the palace until the next day. Zoran wanted to make sure Abby was well rested before transforming again and flying such a long distance. Of course, once Zoran showed her how to transform into her dragon, Zoran's dragon had other ideas and it involved a chase and capture. It was well after dark by the time they arrived and Abby was weak with fatigue. As soon as they landed on their balcony, Zoran swept Abby into his arms before she collapsed into a puddle on the cold stone flooring. He took her to the bath, where he bathed her gently before putting her to bed. Abby remembered very little of it.

It was late morning before Abby woke up to banging on the outer door of the suite of rooms she and Zoran shared. Abby barely had time to get a silk robe on before the doors burst open and Trisha, Carmen, Ariel, and Cara with their respective new symbiot pets came trotting in.

"Good morning!" Cara said brightly as she laid a tray full of food on a low table. "We thought you'd be hungry."

"No, you wanted an excuse to find out what happened!" Trisha said with a grin as she picked up a piece of fruit from the tray and bit into it. "Damn, they have some good fruit here."

"So, tell us all the juicy details. I heard you fried Ben'qumain? How'd you do that?" Ariel said as she laid another tray with cups and a large pot of something that smelled suspiciously like coffee down on another small table.

Carmen didn't say a word but moved over to a chair and sat down quietly, looking curiously at Abby. Abby glanced at the women who had become more like sisters to her. Accepting a cup of coffee from Ariel and a plate of food from Cara, Abby sank down onto the soft cushions of the sofa and pulled her bare feet up under her.

Pushing her hair away from her face, she took a sip of coffee before replying, "I turned, *can turn*, into a dragon."

Abby waited as the news of what she had just revealed sank into the women sitting around her. She glanced at each one under her lashes as she sipped more of her coffee. Ariel and Trisha were staring at her with their mouths hanging open, Cara had a devious grin full of mischief on her face, and Carmen studied her with an expression on her face that Abby couldn't read.

"That. Is. So. Cool!" Cara said excitedly, her voice rising as her excitement grew. "How did you do it? Can I do it? Oh. My. God. I have to be able to do it. I could totally drive Trelon out of his ever-loving, fucking mind! Oh, Abby, you have got to teach me how. Please! Please! Please!"

The three other women glanced from Cara to Abby. Suddenly, a small chuckle filled the air followed by uncontrollable giggling. All eyes whipped around unable to believe where the giggling was coming from.

Carmen wiped her eyes trying to stop giggling, "Oh Abby, please teach us. I would love to be able to give someone else hell, and I'm sure I could think of a hundred different ways to do it in the form of a dragon."

Soon, all the women were giggling and making up ways they could drive the men insane by switching between human and dragon and using the symbiot. Cara's was the most creative but Carmen came up with the most devious. When Zoran walked into the room a couple of hours later and found all five women in hysterics, he had a bad, bad feeling he and his brothers were in for trouble.

* * *

Zoran glanced at Abby, making sure she was comfortable, before he moved over to talk to his brother Mandra. It was the first time they had dined with other males since Abby's transformation and her dragon's first heat. He knew other males would be able to sense what was happening to Abby's dragon and worried. Abby was very sexual, much more so than normal Valdier women. Her dragon would be even more so now that it was going through its first heat and would send out pheromones, letting other males know she was sexually active. Normally, women went through their first heat at a young age, and older females would help guide them through the process, picking out suitable males for the younger females with whom to enjoy their new sexual awakening. Since the females would not reproduce except with the males they would eventually mate with, it gave both the males and the females a chance to sample and enjoy each other. Zoran did not want Abby to sample or enjoy any other males. It was true as a true-mate she wouldn't normally want another male, but he wasn't sure about her feelings while she was experiencing heat. Unfortunately, being in heat meant other males would crave her. He had a feeling he was going to be spending a lot of time fighting off males who would think they were strong enough to take her away from him. He did not worry as much about his brothers. They seemed to be busy trying to mate with the other females who returned from Earth with him. It was all the other warriors on Valdier.

"You okay, Brother? You seem a little tense," Mandra asked as he handed Zoran a drink.

Zoran narrowed his eyes as one of the many males who dined in the large palace dining room moved across to stand close to Abby. "Abby had her first transformation the night she escaped from Ben'qumain. Her dragon is in heat."

Mandra followed Zoran's gaze, frowning, "Ah, this would explain the scent I smelled the last few days."

Zoran's eyes whipped around to face his brother, "You could smell her outside our rooms?"

"Yes." Mandra laughed. "Her scent is very strong. I knew as soon as you were back in the palace."

Zoran growled when he looked back and noticed the male had sat down next to Abby. Abby was trying to scoot farther down the couch only to find another male had come up and sat down on the other side of her.

"I do not envy you. I have enough problems trying to control myself around the one called Ariel. I just don't understand these human females. I let her know I wished to have sex with her, and she said I could, 'Go fuck yourself.' I don't want to do it by myself! That is the whole point of me telling her I wished to have sex with her."

Zoran listened with half an ear as his brother went on to discuss some of the other things Ariel had told Mandra he could do. He could feel the rage building as one of the men put his arm along the back of the couch where Abby was sitting while the other picked up her hand and brought it to his mouth to press a kiss to her knuckles. Zoran had enough when the arm on the back of the couch moved and picked up a piece of Abby's hair to smell it. He felt his dragon's snarl even as the heat began to build inside him.

* * *

Abby pulled on her hand again trying to break the surprisingly strong grip of the man, who had been bothering her for the last ten minutes; she couldn't remember his name. Where was Zoran? He had gone to talk to one of his brothers a little while ago. He should have been back by now, surely! Abby leaned forward as the other man, his name was Buta, put his arm on the back of the couch. She was trying in vain to subtly move away from where he was rubbing his fingers along her shoulder. When he reached over and grabbed a piece of her hair, it took everything in her not to elbow him in the gut. It was one thing for Zoran to put his hands on her, it was quite another for other men. When Mister-I-Don't-Know-Remember-His-Name started tonguing her knuckles, she'd had enough. Standing up, Abby started to move away only to find herself trapped between the two men, one in front and the other behind her.

"Please move away," Abby said quietly, feeling very uncomfortable as more men began to move around her.

"Move or die!" Zoran snarled as he pushed his way into the growing circle of men surrounding Abby.

Zoran wrapped his arm around Abby, growling at the men, "Mine!"

Buta stepped forward, "She is in heat. According to law, any female in heat is available to any male who wishes to satisfy her needs."

Zoran thrust Abby behind his back, "She is my true mate and not subject to the laws of an unmated female."

Another male growled, "I want to fuck her. Share her with us as is our custom."

"Never!" Zoran snarled, his face beginning to elongate as he half shifted to his dragon.

Another male reached over the couch and grabbed Abby around the waist, pulling her up and over against him. Abby screamed and tried to grab for Zoran as a pair of huge arms grabbed her from behind. Zoran whirled around leaping over the couch and slamming his fist into the man's face.

"Mine!" He roared louder.

Abby soon found herself surrounded by Zoran's four other brothers and, to her surprise Cara, Trisha, Carmen, and Ariel. Cara had grabbed a pair of pot lids and was holding them up in front of her; Trisha and Ariel had each grabbed a set of knives off the table and taken a defensive pose as Carmen stood straight, her arms by her side and her feet slightly parted. The expression on her face was scary, as if she were begging the men to give her an excuse to kill their asses.

"Zoran, you better get her the hell out of here until she is finished," Creon said in a low voice, his eyes never leaving Carmen. He growled at Carmen. "Get your ass over here next to me, *now*, Carmen."

Zoran moved slowly back toward the huge double doors, snarling and showing his teeth to any male who moved toward him and Abby. He pushed Abby gently behind him until they were both out the door. Once they were free of the room, Zoran turned and scooped Abby up into his arms and began running for their suite, calling for his symbiot to prepare for both of them. Slamming the door behind him, he set Abby down and bolted the door.

"Go pack a few things. I need to take you away from here for a few weeks," Zoran said darkly as he moved toward their bedroom.

Abby stood in stunned silence for a moment before she followed Zoran. Her gaze followed him as he moved back and forth between their closet and dresser drawers, watching as he pushed items randomly into a large bag. He looked furious as he walked quickly back and forth, muttering curses under his breath.

"What the hell just happened?" Abby asked quietly.

The tendons in Zoran's neck stood out as he fought to control his rage. "You are in heat."

"I'm in *what*?" Abby asked in astonishment.

Zoran looked at Abby, his face softening at the surprised look on her face. He walked over to her kissed her. Sniffing deeply, he couldn't contain the low rumble of his dragon's response to her. "You are in heat, *elila*. You smell so damn good all the males what to fuck you."

"You can *smell* me?" Abby squeaked.

"Oh, yes. And so can every other male within a mile radius. The first heat is the most intense, but it wouldn't matter; they would all still want to fuck you like I want to right now," Zoran moaned quietly as he pressed his hot arousal against the palm of Abby's hand.

Abby blushed a bright red. "They could smell me?" She whispered, her fingers curling around Zoran's hard length.

"Yes. I have to get you away from here until you are finished; otherwise, I will be fighting off every male in the palace."

"Oh."

CHAPTER 23

The trip would take about half a day to get to the mountains. Zoran's mother symbiot had transformed into a type of hovercraft and was waiting for them outside their balcony. Zoran helped Abby into the golden craft, and then climbed in beside her after throwing their bags behind the seats. Abby asked why they couldn't just shift into their dragon forms and fly. Zoran growled that every male capable of shifting would have followed them. He didn't have to explain his fears, the dark look on his face more than told the story of what would happen if they did. They left heading south, but after a short period, Zoran turned them to the west then to the north and increased the speed. He wanted to make sure they wouldn't be followed.

"Where are we going?" Abby asked as she gazed in fascination at the landscape below them.

"To our family retreat in the mountains. Mother lives there now. No one knows where it is except for our immediate family," Zoran said, turning with a small smile. "You know, my symbiot knows where we are going, my hands are free, and you smell delicious. Come, *elila,* sit on my lap."

Abby shook her head. "No way. You may not care, but I do. There is no way I am going to make love to you in this symbiot!"

"Why not?" Zoran asked incredulously.

"Zoran, it's alive," Abby whispered.

Zoran leaned forward and smiled mischievously. "I know," he whispered back.

Abby let out a small gasp as gold straps suddenly appeared around her wrists and ankles. Her seat moved, making a type of reclining bed. As Zoran moved between her legs the straps holding her ankles moved farther apart, giving Zoran more room and forcing Abby's legs apart, as well.

"Zoran!" Abby gasped as she felt Zoran's hands reach under her silk shift to grasp her panties the seamstress had created for her. With a growl, Zoran ripped the panties away.

Zoran threw the destroyed material to one side as he gripped the top of her shift in both hands and ripped it down the middle. "You should not be wearing clothes, especially the garments underneath them. It takes too long to get to you."

Abby arched as the straps holding her wrists move up, forcing her to stretch out fully in front of Zoran. Zoran rose up enough to pull his shirt over his head and release the stays holding his pants on. Pushing his pants down to free his cock, he rose up over Abby, rubbing his cock against her wet clit. With a groan, he pushed the swollen purple head of his cock into Abby's sweet cunt, watching as it disappeared into her. Zoran's whole body shook as he struggled to retain control of his desire. He wanted to take Abby hard and fast, but he wanted her to enjoy it, even more than his own selfish pleasure. His glance flicked up to Abby's face watching as she flushed and pushed at the restraints on her ankles trying to open even farther for him.

"Look at me, Abby," Zoran whispered. "I want to see your eyes as I take you."

Abby's eyes flew open and were snared by the golden glow of Zoran's eyes. Zoran pushed in another inch, watching as Abby's eyes grew larger and heavy with desire.

"No!" Zoran snarled when Abby's eyes started to close. He pulled back until he was almost out, ignoring her whimper. "Open your eyes."

Abby fought to keep her eyes open as the waves of fire began building in her blood. She could feel the heat of her dragon combine with her own desires. Zoran pushed in again, a little farther this time. He snarled something to his symbiot and Abby felt the straps on her wrists tighten and move a little higher, while the ones on her ankles spread her even wider.

"I'm going to fuck you, Abby. For the next two weeks that is all we are going to do. Any way and every way possible. I am going to fuck your tits, your mouth, your pussy, and your ass. I am going to claim you as mine so no other male will ever doubt who you belong to," Abby cried out as Zoran's touch flicked and tasted each part of her as he told her what he was going to do. When his hand slid back up to her stomach he rested it there for a moment. "But most of all, Abby, I am going to plant my seed in your womb. I want you to see who is claiming you, who is loving you, and who the father of your children is as it happens. Do you hear me?"

Abby glared at Zoran. She was incredibly horny and frustrated and all he was doing was teasing her and talking. "Shut up and fuck me, Zoran. Or, find me a male who will."

Zoran growled at the threat of another male, thrusting his cock in hard and fast, pushing it as far as it would go. He felt Abby's climax at the sudden possession and roared in triumph at his domination of her. Ignoring Abby's cries, Zoran rode her, pushing in deeper and deeper, until he could go no further. Abby climaxed again and again, begging Zoran over and over for more. Zoran felt his own release building. He waited until it was upon him before shifting enough to elongate his teeth. Abby arched as if offering her body as a sacrifice, and Zoran bit down on the side of her breast pouring his dragon fire into her. The combination of the dragon fire in her blood and her own dragon's heat caused a wave of desire so intense, Abby screamed in pleasure/pain as it swept through her, locking her in a mind-blowing orgasm that caused her vision to blur and made it difficult to breathe. Zoran's own groan of pleasure/pain followed as Abby's body locked down on his cock, making it impossible for him to withdraw from her, squeezing every last drop of his seed from him and deep into her womb. Zoran felt the precise moment when her womb opened and accepted the new life he was offering. Shudders flowed over him as he pulled Abby close, giving the order for his symbiot to release her so she could wrap her arms and legs around him. They stayed connected until it was time to land.

Abby blushed again as she picked up the scrap of material off the floor of the symbiot and tossed it into the bag Zoran was digging in. He grinned in triumph when he pulled out one of his shirts and tossed it over to Abby. Abby glared at him but pulled it over her head.

"If we meet anyone with me looking like this, I swear I won't talk to you for the next two weeks!" Abby said fiercely as she pulled the shirt down around her hips.

Zoran's grin grew wider. "I plan on keeping your beautiful mouth too busy to be doing any talking, unless it is to talk dirty to me."

Abby just glared over her shoulder trying to keep Zoran from seeing her own silly grin. Damn, but he was an awesome lover. Abby might not have had any experience to compare him to but she honestly couldn't imagine any man, human or alien, who could make her feel so much pleasure she practically passed out from it. Abby ran her fingers through her hair trying to make herself somewhat presentable. She really hoped they didn't run into Zoran's mother before she had a chance to bathe and dress properly. She looked like she had been well and truly made love to. She felt it too! She had to fight with the mother symbiot; then, she threatened the little offspring that appeared around her neck and wrists to *not* move any lower where she was a little sore. The damn thing hadn't listened to her, though. As soon as the seat reformed under her, she could feel it moving between her legs. She screamed and Zoran had the nerve to chuckle as she hit him for laughing at her. He simply said it was the symbiot's responsibility to make sure she was ready for what he planned on doing to her later. After all, he had only fucked her pussy and he had a lot more places to fuck before their two weeks were up. Abby shivered at the thought. What on Earth, or this case Valdier, had she gotten herself into?

* * *

"Abby! Zoran! What a wonderful surprise," Morian exclaimed as they walked up the steps of the most beautiful place Abby had ever seen. The glimmering white building was carved of rich stone with waves of gold and black threading through it. It was surrounded by clusters of large trees that shaded and shielded it on three sides. "Abby, what on Valdier are you wearing? Zoran, can't you even provide the poor child with decent clothing?"

Abby shot Zoran a dirty look and had to bite back a chuckle at watching his cheeks turn a dull red. "Mother, Abby has decent clothing, and she is not a child! Her shift was damaged on the way here."

"Oh dear, how was it damaged? Zoran, you didn't have anything to do with that, did you?" Morian asked with a twinkle in her eye.

Zoran's cheeks turned even redder at his mother's stare, and he mumbled under his breath that he was going to take their bags to the room they would be using while they were there. Morian chuckled as she watched her oldest son scurry away.

"Payback for all the mischief he was in when he was a boy. I swear, it was all I could do not to pull my hair out when those boys were growing up. Now, how about a lovely bit of refreshment while he tries to find the courage to come rescue you from me?" Abby just nodded as Morian threaded her arm through hers and followed the wily woman into a large marble foyer.

* * *

Abby tucked Zoran's long shirt under her legs as she curled them under her. She was very self-conscious about her lack of dress and sure she looked like she had just been made love to. Morian didn't appear to notice as she handed Abby a steaming cup of tea. Morian guided Abby through a large foyer into a room that looked out over a lush garden filled with plants of every color imaginable. No doors or windows blocked the view. The garden was filled with brilliant foliage of many colors, and a small waterfall fell in the background, flowing into a huge basin. Abby had never seen anything so beautiful in her life, not even on her own mountain.

"It is so beautiful," Abby murmured in awe.

Morian smiled as she sat back in her own chair and sipped her drink. "It is. I love it here. I can spend the day in the gardens working with the soil and never tire of it. I can feel the life in it." She glanced under her eyelashes at Abby. "You are in your first heat."

Abby blushed. "So Zoran says. I don't understand any of this."

Morian chuckled. "You have had your first transformation." She said it more as a statement than a question. "This is most unusual since you are not of our world. It appears the stories are true."

"Stories?" Zoran asked, as he walked into the room. He walked over to where Abby was sitting and, without saying a word, lifted her as if she weighed no more than a small doll and settled her in his lap ignoring her squeak of surprise. He wrapped one arm around Abby's waist making sure she could not move and used the other hand to guide the hot drink she was holding to his lips.

Abby's eyes glittered with humor as she watched him take a sip. "You are so bad," she whispered.

Morian watched her oldest son with a satisfied smile before replying. "Yes, stories, legends, tales, prophecy, whatever. It is said that long ago, the first king traveled to a far-off world. The king discovered a primitive world where there were many people. During his time on this planet he was welcomed into a village. While a guest there, he was drawn to one of the females, the daughter of the chief. He was so taken with her, as was his dragon and his symbiot, that he wanted to make her his queen and returned to our world with her. His people were horrified. They feared the female would give him weak offspring as she was much smaller than them, and because she was not a true Valdier, she could never have the power of a true mate, the ability to transform and mate as a dragon and accept the power of the symbiot. It was thought this would weaken the king's lineage and bring death and destruction to the people by angering the gods and goddesses. They demanded the king sacrifice her to the gods and goddesses to show his remorse. When he refused, the people, determined to show the king how weak his off-world mate was, stole her and took her to the cliffs high above where the city now sits to offer her as a sacrifice. The king, furious over having his mate stolen from him, flew to defend her."

Abby was gripping Zoran's arm tightly, her fingernails digging into his flesh as Morian told her story. Abby's eyes grew wide at how much of the story sounded like hers and Zoran's. Of course, the people didn't offer her up as a sacrifice but she had been stolen.

"What happened to her? Was the king able to save her?" Abby asked breathlessly.

Morian's lips curved. "The elder council members had already taken the king's mate to the cliffs and cast her to the ocean below by the time the king arrived. The king, beside himself with grief, swore he would never take another as his, and in his grief, cursed the people of Valdier. Only those who were of royal blood or had found their true mates would be able to give the gift of bearing offspring who would be accepted by the three parts of themselves."

A tear slid down Abby's cheek as if she felt the awful grief of losing her true mate. "What happened to the king?" Abby whispered.

Morian shook her head gently, "Do not cry for the king, Abby. The story did not end there. It is said that the king, in his grief, fell to his knees begging the gods and goddesses to let him join his mate in death. The gods and goddesses, so moved by the great love and grief the king felt for someone not of their world, took pity on him. They realized it was not only his grief but the grief of his dragon and his symbiot calling to them as one entity. They had also felt the grief of the female as she offered herself in exchange for the safety of her mate, begging them to protect him and to forgive his people for their lack of understanding her love for their king. As the king knelt, a great white dragon appeared out of the waves below. As the great dragon landed next to the king, it transformed into the king's mate before the king and his people. The gods and goddesses had given birth to the transformation, the gift of the heat of a dragon's fire to transform a mate into a true mate, one accepted by a Valdier warrior, his dragon, and his symbiot giving her the strength and power of a true Valdier."

Abby sat back in Zoran's arms pulling his arm tighter around her. "Just like what happened to me," Abby said, her face softening.

Zoran wrapped his other arm around Abby to pull her closer. His gaze met his mother's over Abby's head, and he gave her a small smile in thanks. He could feel Abby's total acceptance of him and his world as a peace settled around him. Morian smiled back softly at her son. It was the first time since her own mate died that she felt that she had made the right decision not to join him in death. She could sense the new life in Abby's womb, even as small as it was. She would be needed for many more years to come.

CHAPTER 24

Abby and Zoran spent the next two weeks relaxing. Zoran showed Abby many of the places where he and his brothers used to play as children. He helped her get used to her dragon's needs and desires and showed her how to communicate with her symbiot. Abby taught Zoran how to sing and was teaching him how to play the guitar, which he replicated for her. They spent hours walking through the forests surrounding the mountain estate or swimming in the huge basin in the garden. Abby's favorite time was when they would transform into their dragon forms and fly through the tops of the forest playing chase and capture and making love in both forms.

Zoran came up under the water and wrapped his arms around Abby. They had just returned from another trip of exploring and were enjoying the clear, cool waters of the garden pool. Abby shivered as his warm body pressed against her cooler skin.

Zoran splayed his hand over Abby's stomach. "My son grows in your womb. I can sense him," he whispered as he kissed her damp shoulder.

Abby's breath caught in her throat. "How can you know? Are you sure?" Abby pressed her hands over Zoran's larger one turning to look him in the eye.

"I knew the moment we made him. I felt your womb accept my seed and hold it tight."

Abby's eyes filled with tears. A child. Their child. She closed her eyes trying to use the senses Zoran had shown her over the past two weeks. She focused inward, seeking. She sucked in a surprised breath as she sensed the new life deep inside her. Her dragon was curled protectively around it.

Abby turned in Zoran's arms and wound her arms around his neck, burying her face in his chest. "I can sense it," she whispered softly. She had never felt such a surge of love, or fear, as she did at that moment.

Zoran smelled her fear and pulled her closer to his body. "Never fear, *elila,* I would give my life to protect you and our son. I will do everything in my power to make sure nothing happens to either of you."

Abby looked up. "I know. I love you so much, Zoran, it's impossible to contain."

"I love you more, *elila.*

* * *

Abby waved a tearful goodbye to Morian, getting Zoran's mother to promise to come visit soon. She had many questions. They had shared their news the night before with Morian. She did not seemed surprised at all. In fact, she looked very satisfied. She promised to visit the following month.

The flight back to the city seemed much shorter on the way back. Abby would miss the quietness of the mountain retreat, which strongly reminded her of her own mountain, but she was looking forward to seeing Cara, Ariel, Trisha, and Carmen again. She couldn't wait to share her news with them. She realized she no longer thought of her life before meeting Zoran. She missed Edna, Bo, and Gloria but she felt at home here. Abby looked at Zoran through her eyelashes, studying his strong features. Her heart swelled, as if there was too much love in her to contain it all. Zoran was telling her about his plans to change the spare room into a nursery. Abby sat back and listened to all his plans for the baby trying not to laugh as he talked about making the baby's first sword.

* * *

Zoran gently laid Abby's sleeping form in their bed. It was late, and she had fallen asleep not long before they arrived. He tucked the covers around her and kissed her forehead before heading out to meet with his brothers. He hadn't wanted to worry Abby. He had received a message from Creon late that morning before they left. Raffvin had been sighted by one of Ha'ven's informants heading off world.

Quietly closing the door to their apartments, he ordered the two guards standing outside to guard it with their lives. He called silently to his symbiot to guard the outside balconies. Confident Abby was safe, Zoran moved determinedly toward his office where his brothers waited for him.

"Zoran," Creon greeted him as he entered the room. Mandra handed Zoran a stiff drink as he moved toward the table where they had a holograph image of the planet on display.

"What have you learned?" Zoran asked in a hard voice.

"We received a signal from off world two days ago. From what we have learned, it came from the Sarafin Star System," Creon said, bringing up the holograph of the neighboring star system.

"Sarafin?" Zoran asked with a frown. They had not had problems with the warrior people in that star system for nearly a century.

"Ha'ven believes Raffvin has traveled there to gather supporters to attack our world. The Sarafin are renowned mercenaries," Mandra said. "Our peace with them came at a price; the firstborn daughter of the King of Valdier to wed the firstborn son of the king of Sarafin. Shame we forgot to tell them we usually only have males. Unfortunately, the bastards have a very long memory. It seems a son has been born and they expect you, as the king, to produce the daughter immediately. In the meantime, Raffvin has decided to 'enlighten' them about how unlikely that is to happen and try to get them to believe we have slighted them in some way."

"On top of that, Ha'ven said he still has support on Curizan from the militant group there who wants us to get into a battle with the Curizan warriors. It looks like he is trying to stir up enough conflicts with rival warriors to stretch us thin enough to max out our resources and inflict the most amount of damage," Trelon said.

"The question is why." Kelan said. "Why is he so willing to destroy his own people? What advantage does he have?"

"Luckily, Ha'ven and his brothers seem to be containing the problem on their planet. Now, all we need is for you to produce a daughter and that will defuse the situation with the Sarafin," Mandra said with a grin lifting his eyebrows up and down at Zoran.

Zoran bit back a curse. He knew Mandra was just joking but the idea of him offering up his daughter as a sacrifice for peace did not sit well with him, and he could only imagine the problems he would have convincing Abby he had no choice if their child did, in fact, turn out to be a female.

"Abby carries my child," Zoran said quietly. He sat down heavily in the chair.

Mandra let out a curse. "Zoran, forgive me. I would not have made that comment if I had known."

Zoran waved his hand in dismissal of the apology. "Right now, I need to focus on keeping Abby and the baby safe." Zoran grimaced. "And happy. No one says a word about the agreement with the Sarafin. It will be a mute-point if Abby gives birth to a son. Understood?"

All four of his brothers nodded in silent agreement. "For now, we continue gathering what information we can about what Raffvin is up to. Creon, do you still have an informant inside Raffvin's personal elite force?"

"Yes," Creon replied. "Ha'ven has at least two inside the Curizan. They do not know about each other for safety. Raffvin has tightened his security since one of the spies we had was discovered."

"Then we wait, listen, and plan for any possible scenario. Mandra, you and Creon continue with overseeing the training of the warriors. Kelan, you and Trelon work on making sure all our warships are ready and ground shields are ready in case of an invasion," Zoran said, gazing at the maps before him.

Creon smiled grimly before replying, "You just concentrate on protecting your mate and making sure the council understands the seriousness of the situation."

Zoran smiled. "I think it is time to meet with the royal house of Sarafin. Two can play at the game Raffvin is trying to play. I am, after all, the King of Valdier. Perhaps an invitation is in accord to show our commitment to peace between our two worlds."

Trelon growled low. "You just make sure those horny bastards stay away from the human females. I'll rip every one of their damn throats out if they try anything with my Cara."

Mandra, Kelan, and Creon nodded in response. Kelan added, "I agree. It would not be a good way to establish peace if we have to kill the royal bastards. Maybe we can hide the females."

Mandra and Trelon laughed. "Good luck with that."

Creon just stared down at the table with a fierce frown on his face. His lips tightened with determination. He'd be damned if he'd let another man near Carmen. He'd kill anyone who tried. Of course, knowing Carmen, she would probably beat him to the killing part.

Zoran pushed himself up. Walking toward the door, he had an overwhelming urge to hold Abby close. "We keep a secured open line between us. Trust no one. I'll see you tomorrow."

CHAPTER 25

Zoran nodded to the guards at the door as he quietly let himself into the apartment. Stripping off his clothes as he moved toward the bedroom, he was naked by the time he made it to the bed. Standing next to it, he gazed down on Abby's beautiful face feeling love and wonder rush through him. Pulling the covers back, he eased down next to her trying not to disturb her. He gently pulled her into his arms sliding one of his large hands down to lay it possessively over her still flat stomach.

"You're back. I missed you," Abby said sleepily.

Zoran rubbed his chin against the top of Abby's head. "You should not have even realized I was gone. You should have been asleep, *elila*."

Abby sighed, moving her bare leg up between Zoran's muscular ones. "I love it when you call me that."

Zoran groaned as Abby pressed soft kisses to his chest. The groan turned to a growl when her tongue flicked his nipple. Zoran turned Abby onto her back and pressed her back into the soft mattress as he moved between her thighs. Using one leg, he pushed her legs farther apart as he aligned his swollen cock with her vagina. Pressing forward slowly, he gritted his teeth at the feel of her soft, hot, vaginal walls closing around him. He felt his dragon stir as Abby nipped at his chest and throat playfully. With a soft moan, Zoran buried himself fully inside, and Abby savored the connection he felt with her.

Abby's dragon stretched seductively. Abby felt the playfulness change to hot desire as her dragon demanded her mate. Abby lifted her legs and wrapped them around Zoran's waist holding him tightly against her as her teeth elongated.

Wrapping her arms around Zoran's neck, Abby pulled him closer. "Fuck me," she whispered right before sinking her teeth into Zoran's neck breathing dragon fire into his blood.

Zoran's dragon roared out at the same time Zoran let out a deep growl of his own, his hips jerking in response to Abby's bite. Waves of intense desire engulfed Zoran as the dragon's fire coursed through him. Zoran gasped as the waves built and broke over him. Sweat beaded on his body as the flames scorched him and his cock swelled to the point of pain. Zoran's body thrust forward, impaling Abby.

Abby gasped at the incredible feeling of fullness as Zoran swell inside her. Zoran let out a cry as the wave hit him again. He gazed down at Abby, his eyes glowed a bright gold as he drew back his lips to reveal sharp teeth. He pulled almost all the way out before thrusting forward, moving faster and faster and thrusting so hard Abby had to hold onto his shoulders and squeeze her thigh muscles to avoid being pushed up against the headboard. Zoran gripped Abby's hair in his hands as he continued to thrust, watching as she threw back her head and screamed in climax. Wrapping one hand around the back of her neck, he pulled her up close enough to bite down on her throat near her collar. He held on as he felt his own release wash over him. He had mere moments, before the waves of dragon fire built again. Breathing his own fire into Abby, Zoran watched as Abby's eyes changed to glowing blue flames.

"Now, we fuck," Zoran growled, releasing Abby long enough to pull her legs from around his waist and flip her over. Grabbing her around the waist, he pulled her up onto her hands and knees and mounted her swiftly from behind. Abby screamed as she felt the hard thrust of Zoran's cock pushing through her hot, swollen folds. The fire burned hot and fierce through both of them as they felt wave after wave build and burst over them.

"Mine," Zoran growled deeply; his voice was a mixture of his male self and his dragon. "Mine, forever!"

Abby screamed hoarsely as she came, one climax after another, until she felt that she was going to dissolve into a million tiny pieces. Zoran pushed in one last time before collapsing with a hoarse cry of his own onto his side, his cock pulsing endlessly as he pressed his seed deep into Abby's womb.

Shuddering, Zoran pulled Abby's limp body against his own. "I love you, *elila*."

Abby weakly wrapped her arms over Zoran holding him close. "I love you more, Zoran. I'm glad you abducted me from my mountain."

Abby knew everything would be all right now. She was home. It might be a different world, a different mountain, but she was finally home.

The End

ABOUT THE AUTHOR

Susan Smith has always been a romantic and a dreamer. An avid writer, she has spent years writing, although it has usually been technical papers for college. Now, she spends her evenings and weekends writing and her nights dreaming up new stories. An affirmed "geek," she spends her days working on computers and other peripherals. She enjoys camping and traveling when she is not out on a date with her favorite romantic guy. Fans can reach her at SESmithFL@gmail.com or visit her web site at http://sesmithfl.com.

Additional Books:

Abducting Abby (Dragon Lords of Valdier: Book 1)

Capturing Cara (Dragon Lords of Valdier: Book 2)

Tracking Trisha (Dragon Lords of Valdier: Book 3)

River's Run (Lords of Kassis: Book 1)

Tink's Neverland (Cosmos' Gateway: Book 1)

Hannah's Warrior (Cosmos' Gateway: Book 2)

Gracie's Touch (Zion Warriors: Book 1)

Lily's Cowboys (Heaven Sent)

Preview of *Capturing Cara* (Dragon Lords of Valdier: Book 2)

Synopsis

Cara Truman is a pint-size pistol whose inquisitive nature has gotten her into trouble on more than one occasion. Her next adventure takes her further than she ever expected when she ends up on a journey out of this world.

Trelon Reykill thought he had his hands full. A militant group of Curizans had captured his brother Zoran, and he was busy trying to fortify the Valdier defenses against the Sarafin Warriors, even as his dragon was roaring for him to find a mate. He was furious about the first, excited about the second, and pissed about the last. The last thing he expected to find on the primitive planet his brother has taken refuge on was his true mate.

Now, he has a whole new set of problems...capturing Cara long enough to make her his. His symbiot loves her, his dragon wants her, and he can't catch her. On top of all that, someone is trying to kill her.

His solution: Capture Cara and love her so well she will never want to escape him—if he can.

Made in the USA
San Bernardino, CA
26 July 2015